ARIADNE BREYLARD

SUMMER
KNIGHTS DREAM

Introduction

This Adult Fantasy Romance series is intended for mature audiences and is not suitable for young readers. The characters engage in multiple partner relationships and experience fated mates dynamics (why-choose). These relationships are inclusive, exploring diverse partnerships, including those of the same sex.

If themes such as LGBTQ+, multiple partners, open relationships, or poly are discomforting, it's advised to avoid this book series.

Themes and tropes in this book include: bonded, bullying, cliffhanger, enemies to lovers, fated mates, inst-love, love triangle, multiple POV, other-women-drama, second chance, secret identity, slow burn, smut/sexually graphic scenes with explicit language & description, soulmates, and steamy/suggestive scenes, unrequited love.

This book will end on a cliffhanger.

ARIADNE BREYLARD

SUMMER
KNIGHTS DREAM

To the Night
for making all my dreams come true

Contents

Chapter One

"I'm prey."

"You're not prey." Mother wrapped her hand around my chin and turned my face to look at her. "You're glamoured. That does not make you prey."

"I'm being hunted."

"You're being dramatic as usual, daughter." Father bent down to kiss the top of my head. "You're glamoured in a disguise, not being hunted, and you're certainly not a target. Far from it."

"Think of it as being a coveted prize that the greatest treasure finders are actively searching for." Pai's voice lilted as if he were weaving a tale.

"That's exactly why she's being dramatic, Elio. You make everything fantastical." Baba shook his head at Pai as he caught my eye in the mirror. "You're fulfilling your destiny, as your mother did and your grandmother before her, and so on. This is tradition, my love. This is how you will find mates worthy of the position they will one day hold by your side."

"This is how you will find mates worthy of *you*, my darling," Papa crooned as he hugged me and kissed the top of my head. "I know it feels daunting, but it is necessary."

I sighed and turned to look at myself in the full-length mirror. Tonight, if the fates granted it, I would find my Spring Mate.

The Spring Equinox was upon us, and it was the Spring Court's duty to host the annual mating revelry. Now that I was of age, I was allowed to attend. I was officially being presented to court—not that anyone would know but my parents, my siblings, and the High Priestess. As the heir to the Night Kingdom, my identity would be hidden beneath a glamour and geas so strong that even the High Priestess who placed it couldn't speak of my true identity.

Not even my mates would know who I truly was until they passed a series of magical tests. Acknowledging the mating bond was the first, and the easiest. When they passed whatever tests my magic determined for them, they'd see my true form and be ensnared by the geas, and only after my mating circle was complete would my true identity be revealed to everyone and the geas would dissolve.

Until then, everyone who looked at me would see my glamoured form. I didn't mind my geas form, but I preferred my own features. Under the illusion, my hair was lackluster brown and not the shiny, almost black it truly was. Now, it appeared practically dull. Not terrible, just not what I was used to seeing in the mirror every day for the last twenty years.

My skin, though still smooth, wasn't as creamy or flawless. It was a couple of shades paler and didn't appear as satiny, though it felt just as soft. My brows were rounded, not arched, and my lips were thin and nude rather than their normal blush flushness. My height was the same, though I appeared lankier than I truly was. The only thing that hadn't been altered was the color of my eyes. They were still a silvery violet, though maybe not as bright.

"I barely look like myself," I whispered as I raised my hand to my face.

"That's the point, my darling," Papa said as he stood behind me. Then, with a swift motion of his hand, my glamoured form vanished and I returned to my original appearance. "Remember, only strangers will see your glamoured form. To us, you will always be Lyra, no matter how you appear. We'll see the real you."

I sighed. It was disconcerting to see a face that wasn't mine staring back at me. I was glad I could shift it from my view with a simple swipe of my hand.

"Your glamour is lovely." Father stood in front of me. "Not as lovely as you, daughter, but lovely all the same." He placed a finger under my chin and tipped my head up to smile down at me. "Don't fret. It is not permanent, and the sooner your mates present themselves to you, the sooner your glamour will fall."

"You'll get used to it. Remember, I wore my glamour for over three years before your pai made his acquaintance known." Mother winked at me.

"You wound me, beloved." Pai grabbed his shirt over his heart and dramatically stumbled back.

Mother's first mating bond had emerged at the Autumn Equinox mating revelry, where she'd met my baba, Lugh. Then, she'd met my father, Noel, from Winter and papa, Maxwell, from Spring the first week of her first term at Araphel Academy, where they'd all attended.

The same academy I would attend later this year.

My pai, Elio, had skipped the traditional study of magic and school, and instead embarked on a self-discovery vocation that had taken him across both the Day and Night Kingdoms, where he'd traveled through the seasonal courts of each with a group of free-spirited and like-minded fae. He and my mother had only met by accident at the Beltane festival in the Night Kingdom that mother had been required to attend. Pai and his friends had only been there to restock as they traveled.

"If I had any idea that the love of my life—my fated mate and Queen—was waiting for me at that stuffy academy, I would have sobered up, cut my hair, put on shoes, and marched in there to claim you." He swept her off her feet and twirled her around the room as she laughed.

They were always like this behind closed doors—their true selves. Otherwise, my parents were the prim and proper monarchs of the Night Kingdom the realms were used to seeing. Queen Hesper and her four fated mates and Knight Lords—the noble sons of each seasonal court.

"What's this? Are we having a dance party?" my brother, Puck, cheered as he strode into the room. He ran up to me and swept me off my feet to spin me around the room like our dad was doing to our mother.

My three other brothers, Shea, Tunder, and Cleon, laughed and clapped as they watched. All four of them were older than me, and it was clear which seasonal court and parent they descended from.

Puck was just as free-spirited as our pai, Elio. Shea was as serious as our Winter father, Noel. Tunder was a gentle giant, just like our papa, Maxwell, and Cleon was the smartest of us all, just like baba, Lugh.

"All right, all right. That's enough," Father commanded. "Puck, you'll wrinkle your sister's gown. Please put her down."

"Fine." Puck huffed as he set me on my feet and flung his arm around my shoulder.

Shea winked at me. "You look lovely, squirt."

"We match," Cleon said with a smirk as he put his arm against the bodice of my gown. The fabrics were a similar shade of champagne gold, but I wouldn't say they matched. Sometimes, I wondered if he was color-blind.

"Barely," Tunder jeered.

"They're both yellow."

"That doesn't mean they match."

"It doesn't mean they don't."

"Tunder, Cleon," Baba, our autumn dad, called to them. "We don't have time to debate hues. Now, wish your sister luck. You won't be able to speak with her again until after the ceremony."

My two eldest brothers stopped their color debate and pulled me into a hug.

"I hope your spring mate matches your free spirit, Lyra." Cleon's whiskery chin scratched my exposed shoulder as he spoke.

"Not too free, though." Tunder smirked at me when he pulled back. "You get in enough mischief without any help."

I dropped my mouth open in mock horror. "I do not."

Shea snorted. "Sure, you don't."

"Let's see it, Lala. Show us your glamor so we know who to avoid all evening." Puck pushed himself between Cleon and Tunder as Shea took a position standing next to them.

"You can't call her that either," Mother said as she came to stand next to me.

"Nicknames and endearments were added to the geas, love," Father, our winter dad, told her. "Even if they wanted to, they wouldn't be able to once we leave this room."

"Right." She smiled up at him. "Of course."

"Any last words before you take your first step into adulthood?" Pai teased as he flung his arm around Shea's shoulders.

I worried my bottom lip between my teeth as I looked around at my family. "You'll be able to see me after the party, right?"

They all smiled at me like I was silly, but they weren't the ones being glamoured and hidden from the realms for who knew how long. No one outside the castle knew what I looked like. They didn't even know my name. I was used to being invisible, but this felt different. It was like I was preparing to disappear into the ether.

"Yes, my darling girl, we will all see you at the end of the evening." Baba pressed a kiss to my temple.

I sighed and stood up, straightening my back. "Okay. I'm ready."

Father waved his hand, the glamour slid over my skin like a caress, and the geas that prevented us from speaking about my true identity snaked around my throat like a choker.

Chapter Two

I was warm.

No, my chest was warm.

I wondered if the glass of champagne I'd guzzled was giving me an upset stomach. I probably shouldn't have had anything to drink, considering how nervous I was.

There were still a few minutes before the High Priestess would start the ceremony, so I checked to make sure my family wasn't paying attention and snuck out the side door to get some fresh air. Several fae mingled and drank in the moonlight, and though they didn't look like they were here for the mating ceremony, you could never be too sure. Sometimes, it took a long time to find your fated mate.

Lifting the skirt of my gown, I hurried down the steps.

The air was cooler than it was inside the council hall, but even so, my chest grew tight and my pulse quickened.

What was wrong with me? I sucked in a breath and tried to calm my racing heart.

Was I allergic to champagne? I fanned my face, thankful they'd pinned my hair up. It was thick and hung down to my hips, and if I'd worn it loose, it would've felt like a blanket on my skin.

Maybe a glass of ice water would cool me down? I took a deep breath, lifted my skirts, and turned to go back to the stairs. As I rounded the corner, I ran face-first into a hard chest. My breath expelled from me, and I let out a very unladylike exhale as I stumbled back. A pair of large hands reached out, grabbing my arms to steady me.

"Why are you out here alone?" a deep voice demanded, talking over me as I apologized.

"Sorry, I didn't see you there." My voice sounded off, and it took me all of three seconds to remember why. *Glamour.*

Suddenly, I knew why I felt out of sorts. Why my chest felt tight and my pulse raced.

The male and I sucked in a breath at the same time, just as my heart felt like it was going to leap out of my chest.

His hands tightened around my arms in what I thought was surprise. I was surprised too, and I couldn't help the smile that spread over my face. The mating bond thrummed to life between us, though the ceremony hadn't even begun.

Steeling myself, I lifted my head to look at him.

He towered over me and it felt like I trailed my eyes up his body forever, and even though he wore a noble suit with multiple layers, I could see how muscular he was. He had broad shoulders and a thick neck that led to a strong, stubbled jaw with a light brown dusting of facial hair. His nose was large but proportional to his face. His eyes were an icy blue, surrounded by dark lashes and thick brows that were pulled down in a hard scowl—

Wait.

"Who are you?" the male gritted between his teeth as he shoved me away from him.

I stumbled back several steps and crumbled against the wall.

"I-I..." I stuttered. I was so stunned by his actions that I was at a loss for words.

"Who. Are. You?" The angry male took one long step, glaring down at me. "Why are you here?"

"Mating revelry," I whispered, flinching away from him.

"Leave," he snapped at me.

"Wha— What?"

"I said leave," he sneered, his breaths coming fast and hot as they spilled over my face.

"But ... you're..." My heart banged against my ribcage as the mating bond pulsed between us.

"Nothing." He smacked the wall over my head, and I went still.

My eyes filled with tears as I brought my hand up to my chest. "But ... the mating bond," I whispered as his face drew closer.

"No," he hissed. "Who are you?"

I shook my head. I couldn't tell him who I was. "I'm nobody."

"Exactly. You're nobody." He stood up straight and fixed his suit. "You're weak. I can barely sense any magic from you at all."

"That shouldn't matter," I whispered as I pulled my hands tighter against my breasts.

"I'm a Spring Court noble. I can't be mated to a nobody female with weak magic." He looked me up and down, and for a moment, I thought I saw regret ripple through his features. "The bond you're sensing is nothing." I flinched, and if I didn't know better, I thought he did too. "It's barely there."

"It's not." I shuddered against the agony of my heart thrashing painfully in my chest.

"It is. When the ceremony starts, a stronger bond will remove this ... *thing*, and I'll find my true mate. She'll be the strongest female in the room, just as my parents' seer foretold. Perhaps even the Night Princess."

I jerked at that. This Spring fae thought he deserved to be mated to the Night Princess? To be a Knight of the realms? To *me*? With this attitude?

"You don't know if she's here, or if she's even emerged. Nobody knows anything about her." My voice was marginally stronger as I defended myself.

"Leave," he snapped.

"I can't," I tried to tell him, but he talked over me.

"Don't go into the ceremony. Don't attend another mating revelry. Go home and never return," he bellowed. He looked me up and down, lingering on my face for a few seconds before turning and walking away.

When he was out of sight, the sob I'd been holding in slipped from my mouth before I could stop it. Had my mate just rejected me? Tears tracked down my face. I wiped at them furiously and sucked in a shuddering breath as I tried to regain my composure. My family couldn't see me like this. They couldn't see that I'd been crying. They might expose us somehow, and I couldn't let my identity be known. It didn't matter if my spring mate had rejected me.

I had to go in there. I had to go through with the ceremony.

I had to be publicly rejected in front of my family and the entire assembly by my fated spring mate.

I straightened my back and pulled in a deep breath, filling my lungs to the brim. I wiped my face one last time before drying my hands on my dress. Holding my head high, I walked with purpose up the stairs and through the doors I had exited only a few minutes before. As I walked into the grand ballroom, I ignored the looks I was receiving from my family.

The High Priestess called the room to attention a moment later. The newly-emerged fae gathered around, with the females lining up on one side of the dance floor and the males on the other. I didn't see the male from outside, but it didn't matter. I could feel him nearby. The bond resonated deeply in my core, letting me know he was there.

The High Priestess chanted, and magic flitted through the air until it rose like a great crescendo over the crowd. Excited chatter filled the room as magic swirled around each of us, pulling the mating bond from our center until it was visible for all to see. Males and females alike followed the glowing thread that twirled out from their hearts and linked them to their mates.

I didn't move.

I could feel the heavy gazes of my family as I tried to breathe.

The room erupted into chaos as fae weaved around each other to reach their mate. Those who didn't feel the pull stepped away from the dance floor to make room for those lucky enough to find their match.

I held my ground.

Whispers swirled around me as onlookers wondered why I wasn't moving forward. My hands shook as the chatter grew louder, and my pulse spiked when I saw him moving across the room, following the link that would lead him to me. The magical tie that bound us was brighter than the others', but I knew it wouldn't matter to the Spring Noble. He'd already rejected me, and as far as I was concerned, I accepted it. He couldn't be my mate. He didn't meet the criteria.

He stood in front of me with his hands deep in his pockets. His face was tight as he peered down at me with disdain.

I didn't move.

"I thought I told you to leave."

I drew in a deep breath through my nose and balled my fists.

"Just get it over with," I told him as I stared at the filigree embroidered on his lapel. It surprised me how strong my voice was.

"You did this to humiliate me?" he sneered.

I scoffed. "You're so selfish." I looked up at him then.

His head jerked back at my words. He thought I was weak, so my little comment must have shocked him. His eyes softened as they roamed over my features, then his face went hard again. "You're pathetic."

I gritted my teeth and dug my nails into my palm. I refused to cry in front of this male.

"Do you accept the mating bond?" The words felt like sludge on my tongue.

He drew his shoulders back, trembling as he held himself rigid. "No," he ground out.

My breath caught.

"Do you..."

"No," I whispered as the magic between us faded.

He flinched. My heart felt like it had been ripped from my chest, but I held his gaze for a few moments, then I turned and walked out of the room.

Chapter Three

"Are you sure you have everything?"

"Did you pack the charging stone for your phone?"

"Do you want snacks for your room?"

"Don't forget the fluffy blanket I got you."

"Did you pack extra socks? The floors get cold."

My parents were fretting as they talked over each other.

"I'm fine," I told them as they checked my bags again.

They had been hovering over me since the Spring Equinox. Apparently, watching their only daughter get rejected by one of her fated mates in a public setting made them uneasy.

Shea shook his head as he watched our parents. "She said she's fine."

"Of course, she'll be fine. I'll be there with her." Puck winked at me as he lounged on my bed.

Cleon tried for the third time to get our parents to calm down. "Mother, stop fussing."

"Puck will watch over her," Tunder reassured them.

"I'll be there with her the entire year," Puck said with a nod.

"Of course, you'll watch over her," Father told him sternly.

"But from a distance," Baba reminded him.

"But not so far that something will happen to her."

"Nothing will happen to me."

"Nothing is going to happen to her," Shea agreed, shaking his head again.

Cleon threw his hands up. "You're all being ridiculous."

"Enough!" I stood from the chair. "I know you are worried, but I'm not a little girl. I will be fine. Please stop fussing."

The room deflated with my words. All of my five parents' shoulders slumped as they huffed out a breath.

"Sweetheart, we're just so worried about you after what happened—"

"I know, Mother," I said, cutting her off. We'd been over this. Countless times. "I know you're worried. I understand you're upset. All of you." I looked around the room at each of my family members. As much as my brothers tried to pretend otherwise, they were just as angry about what had happened. "It's for the best. What happened was for the best. Can we please just move on?"

None of them said anything. It wasn't that easy and we all knew it, but voicing it made it real. Instead, I received small nods and placating smiles. It was a start.

"Thank you." I straightened. "Now, can we please go? I have everything I need, and I don't want to be the last one on campus."

"Of course, my darling." Papa stepped forward, and I wound my arm around his.

It had been twelve weeks since the mating revelry fiasco at the Spring Court. After I had left the ballroom that evening, my parents found me in a crumpled mess of tears on my bed. I'd used the portal in our secure suite and traveled home to the Night Kingdom right away. It hadn't been long after my arrival that my parents were there to comfort me. The whole thing had caused quite a stir in the realms.

Evidently, the fae male that had rejected me was the son of one of the oldest noble families in the Spring Court, but they had only recently come into positions of power in the Council. They'd spun the story and convinced half the realms that the rumors surrounding that night were a misunderstanding. They claimed that he couldn't have rejected his fated mate because he hadn't received the calling at all, and the female he'd spoken to was a servant he was comforting after not receiving the mating call herself.

The Queen and Knight Lords' sudden departure was a story in and of itself. There was much speculation as to why they had departed in such a flurry. Some eyewitnesses even stated that the Knight Lords' and their sons had been furious when they left, which was true. They'd all been so upset at having to watch my rejection that they nearly outed me.

Our PR team was much better than the Spring Court's, however. The entire Night Kingdom believed that the Queen, Knight Lords, and their sons—the Night Dukes—had all left as planned. The royal family had informed the Spring Court Council that they wouldn't be able to stay through the evening celebrations as they normally would. The story had been confirmed by the Spring Court noble families, who each released joint statements informing the kingdom of the knowledge. Privately, however, the Spring Court nobles knew very well that the royal family had left abruptly after witnessing the disgrace of a noble son rejecting his fated mate. The crown had quietly admonished the family for such a display and shared their disappointment.

The Queen and Knight Lords had hinted very heavily that the Night Princess wasn't in attendance, and they shared their relief at knowing such a son wasn't the future queen's fated mate. Though the confusion about why he'd done it was left unanswered. They had acknowledged, of course, that everyone had the right to accept or reject the mating bond, and they hoped his decision to do so was for the best.

They'd wished him happiness and peace in his decision. Behind closed doors, however, they had nothing nice to say about him.

I tried my best to avoid it. I still heard more than I wished to, but my family's support and defense of me warmed my broken heart.

The rejected mating bond had been bad enough, but they'd been in an uproar once again when Puck told them that Axel, the Spring Noble who'd rejected me, was a second-term student at Araphel Academy. It had taken all four of my brothers and the High Priestess to convince my parents that getting the noble son expelled from the academy was not in our best interest. They were trying to protect their child, but it was irrational. When they had finally looked at it logically, they'd conceded, though they were still apprehensive about me being near him.

My brother Shea's Divination talent was illusion-casting, and he'd devised a plan to help me. In the weeks after we'd found out I would be attending school with the spring noble, Shea had glamoured himself or one of my other brothers to look like Axel. They'd surprised me at every opportunity, appearing at random to decrease the shock of seeing him. They'd even worn his face as we sat together for meals. Shea couldn't replicate his voice, so the illusion wasn't perfect, but eventually, seeing him had become less difficult. I was almost certain I wouldn't jump out of my skin or turn and run the other way if I was unlucky enough to see Axel on academy grounds.

Shea booped my nose. "Contact us anytime, squirt."

"We'll open a portal, and you can come home," Tunder said, nodding.

"Or we can come to you." Cleon hugged me. "As long as you're alone, of course."

"I'll miss you," I told them as I doled out hugs.

I turned to my dads next.

"We'll have all your favorites for Autumn Equinox." Baba, my autumn dad, smiled at me before bringing me in for a hug and kissing the top of my head. "You're going to do great."

"Thanks, Baba."

"Your brother was correct. You may portal home whenever you want to, my darling girl."

"Okay, Papa," I mumbled into my spring dad's chest as he swaddled me in a tight embrace.

"Focus on your studies, daughter." Father's deep wintery voice rattled through my bones as he hugged me. "Ignore the unworthy male. You're strong, and you will be Queen one day. You already make us proud."

"I love you too, Father," I told him, and he gave me one of his rare smirks.

"Come here." My summer dad pulled me from Father's arms and twirled me around before placing his hands on my shoulders. "Now, promise me you will experiment with all the drugs, drink all the alcohol, and have as much sex as faely possible before you meet your mates?"

My mother gasped, my other dads groaned, and my brothers dissolved into fits of laughter and gags.

"Pai!" I screeched, covering my face as he chuckled.

"E-Elio!" Mother stuttered. "Don't tell her to do drugs!"

"Oh, hush, love. She's going to have plenty of boring things to do. She needs to have fun too!" He pried my hands away from my face. "Experimenting is perfectly safe, and anytime you want to be sober, just use the lustral ring." He tapped the stone on my finger to show me as if I didn't know what he was referring to. "Make sure you cast a coitus care spell when you take someone to bed."

"Elio!"

"Of course, you're decades away from your first heat, but better to be safe than sorry. It's been known to happen. Plus, you don't want to get crotch critters."

"Dad!" I was so embarrassed I thought my face would melt off from the heat of my blush.

He busted out laughing. "It's natural, Lala! Fae are very sexual creatures, and I expect you to make me a granddad someday.

"Oh my gods." I covered my face again. "Can I go now?"

"Yes!" Mother screeched. "By the moon, Elio." She rubbed my back as my spring dad kissed my cheek before letting me go.

"I expect regular check-ins, and if you need anything, you let us know right away. If it's an emergency, you find your brother. Glamour be damned."

"I'll be fine, Mother. I promise. I'll check in. I'll call. I'll text. I'll portal if I need to. I know where Puck's room is, and we worked out a system. I know you're worried, but I'm not a child."

"But you're *my* child." She ran her hand down the side of my face. "I love you."

"I love you too." I pulled her in for another hug.

"Okay! That's enough. Time to go." Puck yanked me out of my mother's arms, gave her a quick kiss on the cheek, and shoved me through the portal.

Puck and I arrived at the school, appearing together in a secret alcove constructed just for us. The windowless room was small for a group of people but large enough to cast a travel portal. It was in a secluded area just outside of the entrance gates to the academy, camouflaged to blend into the natural surroundings and spelled to dissuade curious eyes. We said our goodbyes in private before going our separate ways.

Puck was recognizable for several reasons. He was already a notable student due to him being the youngest son of the Night Queen, but he'd also made a name for himself in his own right. Puck was an accomplished athlete and a champion player for the academy's Starball team. It was his master year too, and he'd made a lot of friends during his time at the academy. So, the chances of him going unnoticed anywhere on school grounds or in the Night Kingdom were slim to none, and him being seen with me wouldn't go unnoticed. Not that anyone would know who I was, but they would certainly look into it.

When enough time had passed, I left the hidden space and maneuvered my way into the crowd, and followed the mass of students making its way to the assembly field.

Araphel Academy wasn't the only school in the Night Kingdom. Each court had a school, and they were all worth attending, but Araphel was the premiere academy. It had a long-standing tradition of educating the royal family and the nobles of the realm, so even though each court had an academy, the nobles sent their heirs to Araphel. They all hoped their progeny would meet—or be the fated mate of—the Night Princess or the Night Heirs.

Each of my brothers had found one of their fated mates. I'd never met them officially, though. They weren't allowed to know who I was until the geas was lifted.

Shea, my winter brother, had met his mate during his second year at the academy when she'd arrived for her first term. He'd been certain she was his only mate, and she had felt the same. Single matings were rare, and they'd gained some notoriety when they'd announced their bond status to the kingdom. Shea had been annoyed by the extra attention, but we'd all thought it was exciting.

Tunder had met one of his mates at the Autumn Court mating revelry. The female had worked for the Autumn Court nobles and hadn't been there as an official participant, but the bond had been strong and they'd found each other. They both swore that there'd been another bond present that night, but neither of them had ever found the person. However, they were certain there was another mate in their bond group.

Cleon had met his mate after he'd fallen during a rock-climbing accident while visiting the spring court. It had been a bad enough injury that his magic hadn't been healing his wounds and he'd needed a healer—who had ended up being his mate. Both believed they had another mate too.

Puck had met his mate at the academy last year when he'd transferred from another school. They were roomies this year in the mated dorms because of it, which was another reason he was so eager to get back to school. They hadn't seen each other over the summer as much as he would have liked.

Knowing how many mates you had or where they were and what court they came from was anyone's guess until your first was presented. Unless you were the ruling queen. Fae society was matriarchal, and each queen had a minimum of four mates—one from each seasonal court. There were only a handful of times in history that a queen had more than four mates. The very first Night Queen had eight—six Knights and two Ladies. She was the most notable, but it had been known to happen, though it is the exception and not the rule. My great-great-grandmother had had five mates. One of her Knights had died in battle, and during his memorial, she'd met his twin sister for the first time and they'd been revealed as mates.

I'd always found it fascinating that the ruling queens had more fated mates than any other fae, but after being rejected by my spring mate, I was nearly obsessed. And hopeful. And worried. Would I be the first queen with only three mates? What would happen if the others rejected me too? Would I find another spring mate now that I'd been presented? Or would I have to wait until the next spring ceremony? How would this affect my ability to produce an heir of my own?

The magic woven into my birth and bound to my position was unparalleled. As the progeny of the night queen, I was uniquely equipped to maintain balance in my kingdom when I ascended to the throne. I was the daughter of night, imbued with the power of darkness and magical energy of the elements. Although I lacked the full potential of any particular season's power, my mates would compensate for this, making our bond crucial for the well-being of our realm.

However, my rejected status was unprecedented—at least, to my knowledge—and I couldn't help but fear what it would mean for my kingdom's future.

I sucked in a breath and shook myself out of my spiral, and focused on where my feet were taking me. That line of thinking had been the sole reason for my sleepless nights, and I refused to succumb to my dark thoughts any longer.

When I reached the assembly field, I took the first seat I came across. I knew the student body was large, but I hadn't realized how many fae were in attendance. I was totally alone, and looking around, it became even more apparent. Luckily, I didn't mind being isolated.

As the seats filled, the students chatted with each other until the headmaster appeared in the middle of the assembly. Everyone stilled and went quiet with his arrival.

"Welcome to Araphel Academy." His deep voice rumbled through the crowd. "I am Headmaster Thornweald. Here, you will learn to control your magic properly, ethically, and morally. You'll study and understand your shifted forms, and you will discover and master your imperium talent." He lifted his hand, and with a single wave, magic filled the air. An icy chill tingled around my wrist. I looked down to find a thin, almost glowing green line circling the once-unblemished skin.

"The wristlet will identify your Elemental Magic. If you do not have a wristlet, you may not have discovered your element yet. This is not a test of strength or an indication of power; it is simply an identification marker for you, your professors, and your peers. As you gain power through study, you may find yourself with more but never less."

The foundation of Elemental Magic was rooted in the elements of earth, wind, fire, and water. To wield Elemental Magic, a user had to have a source of power to draw from. This could be a natural resource or a personal source, such as a special object or talisman that resonated with the user's elemental affinity. Some would have access to only one element while others could have two or even three. Though their wield strength for the additional elements varied. Only the Queens of the realms and the Princess heirs possessed all four elements.

An Imperium Magic was the mastery of one's Elemental Magic and didn't require a source to be conjured.

"This is your Divination Sigil." Headmaster Thornweald lifted his hand again, and with it came another cool tingle, this time on my opposite wrist. "This symbol indicates your Divination order. It will allow you to come and go from the academy, starting now. Once you've completed your studies, the wristlet and the sigil will be removed."

The sigil that appeared on my inner wrist was about the size of a coin. All the sigils started with a triangle. Sensory had two triangles mirroring each other to create a small diamond in the middle. Affliction was a single triangle with two straight lines across the middle. Psyche, which was the symbol on my wrist, was a triangle with a small circle around the top. When they were all stacked together, they formed the Araphel Academy Sigil.

Unlike elemental magic, which was tied to the physical world and the elements that made it up, Divination Magic was metaphysical. This magic was of the mind, body, and spirit, and was categorized into Psyche, Affliction, and Sensory.

Psyche could include a wide range of abilities, from telepathy and mind-reading to sensory manipulation, astral projection, and more. Affliction could manifest physically as well and could include teleportation, invisibility, and camouflage to physical manipulation. Sensory was more spirit-based, but the wielder could also affect the physical, including portal creation and illusion magic to tracking, summoning, and even emotional manipulation.

One of the key aspects of Divination Magic was its subtlety and versatility. Unlike the more obvious displays of elemental magic, which often involved the manipulation of physical objects or the creation of elemental forces, Divination Magic could be wielded without anyone else even knowing it was happening.

However, the use of Divination Magic could also come with significant risks and drawbacks. The metaphysical was a complex and delicate thing, and the use of Divination Magic could have unintended consequences, including memory loss, emotional instability, and even permanent corporal damage. As a result, those who wielded this powerful and potentially dangerous form of magic had to do so with caution and care, balancing the potential rewards of their abilities with the very real risks involved.

"Updated class instructions are being sent to you now," he said, and my cell buzzed in my pocket.

I pulled out the thin device and clicked on the link that appeared on the screen. It took me to the page that listed my classes. My name was at the top, along with three symbols that categorized my magic. One of the symbols matched the one inked on my inner wrist to show my Psyche Divination Magic. I didn't fully know all the talents I had yet, but I knew I would soon find out through my studies. One of my abilities was astral projecting, but I was still learning and didn't have access to more than that. The other symbol was a circle with an unfinished symbol inside. It represented my Imperium Magic, which was my shadow magic. This symbol wouldn't show clearly until I was released from the geas and could claim my identity. Until then, everyone would just assume that I hadn't manifested that ability yet.

Last was a green line, which represented my earth element. Even though I had power in all four, there was only one on my wrist and the screen.

Peeking at my neighbor's cell, I noticed symbols for her Elemental Magic and her shifted form at the top of her class schedule. As far as everyone else knew, I didn't have an Imperium Magical talent for any Elemental Magic, and I didn't know what my shifted form was. But I did—it was also hidden beneath my glamour. When I shifted from fae to shadow, my form was called a Nightshade.

I could take any shape, becoming as small as a woolly aphid or larger than a dragon. I could blend in with the dark and control shadow.

I was the embodiment of night, and just like my shifted form, I had to keep that knowledge in the shadows.

I crossed my fingers I wasn't the only one without a shifted form to speak of, or it would be yet another thing that singled me out and made me different.

When everyone had received their updated class schedules, Headmaster Thornweald went over the festivities calendar. On my cell, another link appeared with a list of all the approved parties, holiday socials, and school events on campus.

The cheerleaders bounced across the grass and did a routine before lining up to welcome the Starball players. The coach announced the newly appointed captains, and I wasn't surprised to learn that Puck had been named Captain of the Silver Squad. His mate, Roko, was Captain of the Black Squad.

They all played for the same team, but I chuckled at the rivalry that would inevitably pit the offense and defense squads against each other. They were already teasing each other onstage, but it was all in good fun.

The new players were introduced next, and I was surprised when Axel—my rejected spring mate—was announced for the Black Squad as their Star Kicker. I'd discovered enough about him to know he was on the Silver Squad last year. I squinted at Puck, positive he was the reason Axel wasn't on his team any longer. He wasn't supposed to be meddling.

As if he felt my glare, Puck found me in the crowd and winked in my direction as his lips fought a smirk.

The girl next to me sucked in a breath and snapped her head toward me. "Did you see that?"

Confused, I turned to her and noticed the blush creeping up her neck before flushing her cheeks.

"The Night Duke just winked at me," she squealed.

I couldn't hold back my giggle as I nodded. It was a better story than the truth, anyway, so I'd let her believe he was looking at her. "I did see that."

"Oh my gods, do you think... Could he be my mate?" Her eyes were wide as she turned to look at Puck.

The players laughed and shoved each other around on the platform after the introductions had been made. Puck pulled his mate against him and wrapped his arms around Roko's waist as some of the other players shook their hands.

"Maybe." I shrugged at the girl, but I ignored her excited wail as I stared at Axel. My eyes continued to seek him out without my permission. He was scowling at Puck and Roko, with his thick arms crossed over his chest.

His dark blond hair was styled the same way it had been when he'd ripped my heart out. It was short and combed to the side, every strand impeccably arranged. He had the perfect dusting of facial hair from an intentional missed shave or two. His features were hard, his jaw was bunching as he seemed to grind his teeth, but his lips looked soft even though they were pursed in annoyance. He was taller than most of the other players, his shoulders wider. He was obviously strong and toned with brawny muscle.

Why did he have to be so handsome? Wasn't it bad enough that he'd rejected me? I had to be attracted to him on top of it?

"Jerk," I whispered before I could stop myself.

His back straightened, and he began scanning the stadium as if he'd heard me. I ducked my head and shuffled through the bag at my feet, hoping he didn't see me. There were several hundred students in the arena, but I wasn't willing to risk it.

The girl next to me sucked in another breath. Her eyes went wide and the blood drained from her face, leaving her pale.

"Are you all right?" I asked from my crouched position.

"I..." She shook her head as she stared straight ahead, unblinking. After ten agonizing seconds, she released her breath and slumped in her chair. "I think the Black Squad's Star Kicker was glaring at me."

I groaned. The poor girl was getting all my unwanted attention, and I couldn't even correct her.

"I hope he's not my mate." She sucked in a shaky breath.

Why did she think all the males who looked at her were her mates? I bit back a smile. She was adorable in a silly, naïve kind of way. She seemed even more sheltered than me, and I had basically been sequestered my entire life.

"Do you think..." She looked down at me as if I held all the answers. "They both just looked right at me! Is that how it works?"

I shrugged my shoulders. "I don't know for sure, but I don't think so." I couldn't tell her I knew, obviously, but I hoped my doubt was enough to ease her mind.

"You haven't found any of your mates either, then?"

I held back a wince and pivoted away from her. I would have told her the truth, but my cover story relied on the Spring Court's claim that I'd never been rejected by the jerk onstage.

"No," I shook my head and whispered, keeping my focus on the items in my bag.

She hummed and gathered her things as the assembly was dismissed. We made our way to the aisle, and she fell into step beside me.

"I'm Callie, by the way." She held out her hand, and I took it with a smile.

"Lyra," I replied, and her eyes lit up.

"That's such a pretty name!"

Chuckling, I pulled my hand free of her grip since she didn't seem inclined to release it. "Thank you. You have a lovely name too."

She rolled her eyes. "I'm from the Summer Court. My mother named me after a flower, which isn't very original."

I grinned. "It's still a nice name."

We continued to move in the same direction, and when we took our third turn together, we looked at each other and laughed.

"Are you going to the earth dorms?"

I lifted my wrist to show her my earth band. "I am."

I could've gone to any of them, but I chose earth when we'd been deciding what parts of my magic to reveal while I was in attendance. I loved spending time in the garden and growing things with my magic, so earth had been an obvious choice.

"Oh, maybe we're neighbors," she squealed, pulling out her cell.

I knew we weren't, but I pretended to check my assignment anyway. I had been placed in a suite at the end of the hall, and the two rooms closest to me were "filled" but unoccupied.

"What's your floor? I'm room sixteen on the third floor."

"Bummer." I turned my cell to her. "I'm on four, room twenty."

"Dang," she grumbled, stuffing her cell in her pocket. "We can still hang out, though."

I smiled at her. "I'd like that."

"Great! I'll get settled and come up to your room before dinner. We can go to the dining hall together," she announced, looping her arm through mine as we walked through the main doors.

We rode the lift upstairs, and she pulled me against her in a sort of arm hug before releasing me.

I waved to her when she stepped off on the third floor, and hurried to my room. As I closed the door behind me, I smiled, grateful for the small gesture of affection. Thanks to Callie, in this moment, at least the world didn't seem quite so scary or uncertain anymore.

Chapter Four

My bags were waiting for me in my dorm. Each room on campus was exactly the same, so it wasn't anything special. But it was nice. The bedroom and ensuite were separated from the small living space, and there was a little kitchenette with a window that looked out into the forest. My room at home had a balcony that faced the forest, so my parents had picked this room for that reason. Each of my windows here had a comforting and familiar view. I quickly unpacked and when I finished, I sat at my desk to review my schedule. I'd received my classes and a map of the campus weeks ago—which I'd already memorized—but I pulled it out again to make sure nothing had changed. Of course, it was all the same. I was just being paranoid.

A short while later, an excited knock startled me, even though I had been expecting it. I opened the wooden barrier to a beaming Callie. She was still in casual wear from earlier that was similar to mine. Jeans, a t-shirt, and sneakers. Her shirt was a graphic tee with a psychedelic mushroom smoking a joint on it.

Her curly brown hair was pulled into a high ponytail, making a sort of halo around her head. It was cute. Layered through the color were streaks of lighter browns, blonde and auburn. She was pretty and looked innocent and sweet with her freckles, button nose, and plush lips. But I could sense a strong personality and confidence within her.

I'd changed and had on a plain white shirt that matched my plain white shoes and light-colored jeans. My hair was loose and smoothed straight, hanging down the length of my back.

There were certain aspects of my appearance I'd been able to keep. That way, when I was finally revealed from my glamour, it wouldn't be such a difference. My hair was one of them, and I was happy to have it. I was still getting used to the slight tone difference in my voice, but I didn't see the rest of my glamour, so I wasn't bothered as much about my visage as I'd thought.

"Ready?" She beamed.

"Yes." I stepped through the door and locked it behind me.

She told me about what she'd been doing the last couple of hours and how she'd rearranged her room to fit all her belongings. Then she mentioned her neighbors, who were apparently annoying and cliquey. She rolled her eyes as she relayed their interactions.

"Can you believe that? We're not thirteen-year-old girls in grade school—we're adults at an academy. You'd think the mean girls' BS would have been phased out by now, but apparently not."

Watching her, I chuckled at her dramatic reenactment of the conversation as we walked through a set of double doors that led toward the dining hall.

"Oh no!" She grabbed my arm, pulling me to a stop. "Don't look, but the Star Kicker is at the end of the hall."

My back tensed, but I smiled at her. "We're just going to walk by. Keep talking to me, and keep your eyes straight ahead. You don't know him, he doesn't know you, and there's no reason to hesitate or interact," I told her, reciting my mantra to her. "Indifference is key. He's nothing."

She nodded and pulled in a breath, then she straightened her shoulders and continued down the corridor. Though I'd been desensitized to his face thanks to my brothers, my heart beat faster knowing it was actually him and not a glamour. Luckily, he hadn't noticed either of us. He leaned against a wall, laughing with a group of guys in conversation.

Callie had gone back to her story, and if I didn't know better, I would've thought she hadn't even seen him. She was an amazing performer, and I was sucked back into her tale in no time.

I tried my best to ignore the lingering tug in my chest, but with each step in his direction, the pull grew stronger. I didn't know how long a broken bond would take to fully heal, but I hoped it was soon. The ache in my heart was painful, even more so than it had been the entire time after he'd rejected me.

"What the fuck?"

As much as I didn't want to recognize that voice, I did. It had ripped my heart out only months ago.

Callie's steps faltered, and she stuttered over her words. I hooked my arm through hers and pulled her down the hall.

"Almost there. What did she say after you called her a snobby bitch?" I hugged her arm, the same way she had hugged mine after we first met.

She looked up and gave me a grateful smile, diving right back into her story. I nodded along and took the lead. I looked away from her and steered us around the offending male. He was turned toward me with his arms crossed over his chest, and a familiar scowl was carved into his face. Which was the only look I'd ever known him to have for me.

We were only a few steps away. His buddies looked between us curiously, focusing on me and Callie as we approached.

Axel sneered. "Why the fuck are you—"

I didn't look at him. I could see him, but I didn't look at him. His words cut off as I continued past as if he hadn't said a thing to me. As if I didn't know exactly what he was saying and to whom he was saying it to. He'd rejected me. He was nothing to me—he'd made sure of that. Why the fuck would I give him the time of day?

Callie was still talking when I opened the door, and I ushered her inside before following her into the dining hall. Neither of us gave them another glance.

"Uh..." I heard one of his buddies ask, "What was that about, Axe?"

Another started howling with laughter. "Whoever she was, she couldn't give two fucks about you!"

They all chuckled, and I heard the distinct sound of a hand slapping someone's back. "Come on, let's—"

The words were cut off when the door closed, and at the sound, Callie released a breath and the tension in her shoulders.

"I think he was going to yell at me."

I gave her a sad smile, wishing I could tell her the truth. "I don't think he was going to say anything to you, Callie. You don't know him, remember? He's probably just some random jerk."

She made a noncommittal noise as she nodded her head. "Yeah, maybe. I do have an overactive imagination." She laughed at herself.

We grabbed plates of spaghetti and breadsticks, and found an empty table. Callie took over the conversation again, allowing me to relax. We were nearly finished with our food when a booming laugh and a loud squeal echoed around the room.

I recognized the laugh. I shouldn't have, but I did.

My stomach soured, and I pushed my plate away. I was no longer hungry. "Are you almost finished? It's been a long day."

"Oh yes, I'm ready." She wiped her mouth. "I'd love a hot bath and an orgasm before bed," she announced as if that was a totally normal thing to say at the dinner table.

I snorted at her but didn't respond. We picked up our plates and took them to the depository before weaving our way through the tables as we headed for the exit.

Axel was seated at a table near the doors. He was surrounded by a group of people, and a blonde female was perched on his lap.

"Come back to my room," he said, loud enough for Callie and me to hear as we passed. "You can bounce that ass on me without these clothes on."

"Axel, it's late," she whined.

The weight of the door slammed behind us, cutting off the rest of her sentence. That door was becoming my best friend at the academy—second to Callie, of course.

"Gods, he's a louse." Callie wrinkled her nose.

"Yeah, he's a real jerk," I agreed, willing my heart to stop breaking apart in my chest.

She sighed and looked over at me. "At least he's not my mate. I've felt nothing but annoyance toward him. That's not how the bond works, I'm sure of it."

I smirked and threw my arm around her shoulders. "If being annoyed at a jerk was how the mate bond worked, we'd all have a hundred."

She snickered. "Gods, could you imagine? Ugh. I don't have that many holes!"

A hearty laugh burst from my mouth, and she joined in with one of her own. She kept up with that train of thought as she tried to work out the logistics of sex with multiple mates, deciding that three holes and two hands were more than enough to get the job done. That was until her over active imagination kicked in and she wondered what other parts of her body she could use.

Despite being utterly ridiculous, it served as the perfect distraction from both my broken heart and the male who was responsible for it—the one I had left behind with my half-eaten spaghetti.

Chapter Five

The school uniforms were as awkward as I'd expected. I was an adult, yet I had to wear the same outfit as the entire student body. It was weird. Dress slacks were an option for female students, but I opted for a skirt. They were traditional school uniforms. The skirt was black with silver pinstripe. I paired it with a white button-up shirt and a simple crossover tie that matched. White knee-high socks and chunky-heeled loafers finished off the look. I left my hair down and applied a light dusting of makeup, then I grabbed my shoulder bag and stepped into the hall.

The corridors were busy as everyone rushed around, going for the stairs or elevator, or even using the open doors to leap out if they had magic or a shifted form that allowed them to do so.

My first course didn't start for another hour, so I took a chance and knocked on Callie's door to see if she had time for breakfast. We hadn't compared schedules yesterday, and I found myself wishing we had.

She swung the door open with a smile on her face. "I was hoping it was you! Do you have time for breakfast?"

My lips tipped up. "That's what I came to ask you."

"Awesome," she sing-songed as she grabbed her bag and slammed the door behind her. "What's your first class?"

"Economics."

She wrinkled her nose. "What? Why?"

"Business degree."

"That's so ... normal." She shook her head. "I thought you'd say something cool, like botany or geology."

I raised a brow. "Geology is cool?"

She chuckled. "You have earth affinity. I just assumed it would be something related."

"What are you studying?"

She rolled her eyes. "My parents want me to take over the family business, so I'm here for Phytotherapy."

"A doctor?" My eyes widened. "That's amazing, Callie!"

She shrugged. "I have healing magic, too, so it sort of makes sense. And I love plants." Her eyes grew bright. "But, like, not normal plants. I have a dragon fruit mushroom tree in my room. You should come check it out later."

"A what now?"

"I can't explain—it's better if you see it. But the fruit is amazing!" She laughed, then scrunched up her nose again and looked at me. "Isn't Economics second year?"

Pinching my lips, I flicked my eyes to her. "Advanced placement. I'm doing a dual major in Philosophy and Economics, in addition to our Fundamental Magics."

"So, three degrees." She tilted her head and smirked.

"Fundamental Magic doesn't really count since it's required, but I suppose three. Yes. And you're doing two by that logic."

She slipped her arm through mine and squeezed. "I knew we were going to be besties. Smart and hot, just like I like 'em."

I blushed at her words. I couldn't help it. I didn't think my glamour was all that hot. It wasn't unattractive by any means, but it wasn't really me.

I let that thought trail off for multiple reasons. I was still hurting over being rejected, and he was my professor! I was a secret princess and the future Night Queen, but that didn't mean I was celibate or a blushing virgin. I just didn't think mixing business with pleasure was a smart thing to do on my first day.

Still, we eyed each other for a few moments before someone cleared their throat behind me. I smiled as Professor Warrock gave me a wink, and I turned to find a seat.

I didn't let my smile drop when I found myself face to face with Axel—I just side-stepped him and went to the other end of the room, and took a seat. I considered finding a spot at the back, but now that the hot teacher had winked at me, I decided the front row was a better choice.

I sat at the end of the row and pulled a notebook out of my bag. Professor Warrock moved behind his desk as he continued to check in students, but after each one, he flicked his eyes in my direction. I saw a little smirk play on his lips each time he caught my eye.

All the while, the Spring Noble who'd tossed me away like yesterday's trash without so much as a conversation was scowling at me from the other side of the room. His glare was like daggers in my skin, and the way he clenched his jaw looked like it hurt.

The space in my heart he should have filled was aching, but I pulled in a deep breath and ignored the pain. I knew the last remnants of the link would fade away eventually, leaving nothing between us, but I didn't understand why it was still there. Everything I'd ever been taught—and everything I'd researched after the fact—said that as soon as we rejected the bond, the magic would be severed.

However, the research was a theory at best and seemed mostly speculative since mate rejection rarely happened. The study was based on mates who'd met but couldn't complete the bond before one of them passed away. But the accounts were skewed because they hadn't rejected the bond, but they just hadn't completed it. So while they hadn't felt the pull, they'd still missed their mate. It was all very confusing.

When the last person took their seat, Professor Warrock started his lecture. Thankfully, I was well-versed in the lesson. My parents had hired private tutors for their children long before we could walk. I didn't think I knew enough to test out of my classes, and my degrees required attendance anyway, but I was relieved I wouldn't struggle with my studies. Still, I diligently took notes and listened with rapt attention.

And if it gave me an excuse to look at the handsome teacher, so be it.

Ever since the Spring Court's mating revelry, I'd been worried about the parts of the mating bond that hadn't been severed, but I never considered those that had. If we'd accepted the bond that night, I wouldn't have found Professor Warrock charming and handsome. A mating bond would have formed, and I would only have had eyes for my mates. Since I wasn't bonded, I could still find other males attractive.

The thought shouldn't have brought a smile to my face, but it had. I bit my lip to hold it back, blushing as I looked down at my paper. I had been heartbroken since I'd left the equinox that night. My insides still ached at the rejection, and if I focused on it—or the brooding male who was still glaring at me from across the room—the pain took my breath away.

But it was fading ... slowly setting me free.

Class let out a short while later, and I felt lighter as I moved to the exit.

"See you next week, Ms. Bruadar." Professor Warrock's voice was like a caress over my skin.

I turned to find him staring at me, and I smiled as I pushed through the door.

I made it out into the hallway and around the corner before a hand wrapped around my upper arm and pulled me into a dark room.

Chapter Six

A shadowy figure shoved me against the wall as the heavy door slammed shut with a bang. A lamp flickered to life in the corner and gave me a clear view of the jerk who had grabbed me.

"What the fuck are you doing here?" Axel hissed, towering over me.

I dropped my hands from where I'd held them against my chest and stood up straight, clenching my fists. "Who the hell do you think you are, grabbing me?"

He looked a little taken aback, but when I went to shove him away from me, he grabbed my hands and pinned them to the wall.

"Who the hell am I?" he snarled. "Who the hell do you think I am?"

I squinted up at him. Was he serious? "You're nobody," I whispered.

He jerked away from me, dropping my hands and stumbling backward. I rubbed my wrists where he'd held me. He hadn't hurt me, but the memory of his touch was burned into my skin. He tracked the movement, and a flash of regret flitted across his face. But it was gone in the next blink. As he'd always done before, he shut down and his mouth twisted with a scowl once again.

"Why are you here?"

I rolled my eyes and adjusted my bag. "I'm here for the same reason as you, and if you can't figure that out, then you're in the wrong place."

I spun on my heel and reached for the door, but Axel smacked a hand against it, holding it shut. He was close enough that I could feel the heat of his body behind me.

"You shouldn't be here." His cool breath tickled my neck as he spoke, and I shivered. "You need to leave before you get hurt."

That made me stiffen. "Are you threatening me?" I turned my head to look at him, and my nose brushed against his.

He glared down at me, but he didn't move. Instead, his eyes flicked to my lips. "Not physically."

"Then you're in luck. You've already done your worst."

His teeth snapped together, and before he could say more, I turned away and elbowed him in the gut. I knew I shouldn't have, but I also threw some magic behind the blow, so he flew back several feet—enough for me to open the door and escape.

I heard a loud bang behind me, like a fist punching into something, before the familiar sound of a door slamming.

"This isn't the place for you, little nightmare." His voice carried down the corridor, following me as I rounded another corner.

I didn't want to cry, but his words hurt. I couldn't believe just a half hour ago I'd been smiling about how he wasn't affecting me. I wanted to kick myself as hot tears tracked down my face before I could wipe them away. I slipped into the ladies' room and shut myself in a stall, hiding my face in my hands and collapsing on the toilet to cry.

I'd spent my entire life fantasizing about meeting my Knights. I'd always imagined they would be happy to meet me, doing anything and everything to pass their mate challenges. They would vow to protect me and love me unconditionally, and when they'd learned the truth, they'd be excited about our future together.

Never in my wildest dreams had I imagined being rejected.

I'd never considered that one of my Knights would fail his first test and toss me away, dismissing our bond because I wasn't powerful enough.

Bonds were common. They were special, but everyone had one. Still, you didn't throw them away. You didn't break your bond over social standing, looks, or abilities. That was ridiculous.

Even though all fae found their mates eventually, it could still take years before you found your true love. Why would anyone throw that away? Why would you break the very essence of being a fae? Aside from our magic, our mating bonds were an inherent gift from the goddess.

I didn't understand why Axel had refused me. Why he thought he deserved more than the gift of a mating bond. He'd broken my heart, but why was he being cruel to me on top of it? What had I ever done to him to deserve such treatment?

Other than not being who he'd thought I was.

I only hoped that when my other Knights were revealed, the bond between Axel and me disappeared entirely. Because when he learned the truth of who I was—the exact person he rejected me for—I didn't want to feel anything other than satisfaction. He'd failed his first mating test, and the very thing he thought was more important than love was the one thing he would never have.

He could have been my first Knight, which was an honor in itself. He could have helped me rule the kingdom when the time came for me to ascend. He could have fathered the next Night Queen and a child of his own. A Night Duke or Lady.

If he'd accepted the bond, we might have progressed far enough for him to know my true identity by now. We could have been living together on campus in mated quarters.

But he'd made his choice, and it was his mistake to live with.

I angrily wiped the tears from my face and blew my nose before pulling out my compact. My eyes were bloodshot, and my skin was blotchy and puffy. Even my nose was red.

"No more, Lyra," I chided my reflection.

Waving a hand over my face, I fixed my makeup and healed my appearance. Aside from the thickness in my voice, no one would know I'd been crying. I washed my hands and left the ladies' room, officially running late for my next class.

I refused to let him hurt me any more, and I certainly would not let him affect my studies or my time at the academy. If he didn't want me, that was his problem, but I had every right to be here, even *if* I wasn't the Night Princess. He would just have to ignore me because I wasn't going anywhere.

Chapter Seven

It was frustrating to learn that due to my advanced placement, I had more than one class with Axel.

On my first day of classes, I'd had Economics with the moody male. The next day, we'd shared Business Studies and Elemental Earth. On day three, I hadn't see him at all, which had been a relief. I hadn't had any official classes with him on the fourth day, but he'd joined my Earth Grounding session during Rejuvenation hour—one of the many optional classes we took to replenish our magic. I'd chosen to do an Earth Grounding session, which evidently, he had chosen to. It made sense since one of his Elemental Magics was earth, but it didn't curb my annoyance. By the fifth day, I had to bite back a scream. He was in my Divination Psyche class and my Rejuvenation hour, Water Natant.

Even though I was only exhibiting one elemental wristlet, I held all four elemental powers. All fae drew replenishment and energy from the different forms of Gaia, but it was more common to draw directly from your elemental source. I.e., water from water, earth from earth, etcetera. So, like everyone else, I could replenish with any element but enjoyed sourcing from them all, and I'd chosen Rejuvenation hours that did just that.

"So, I've been thinking about our first day," Callie said, breaking the comfortable silence we'd been sharing for the last twenty minutes or so.

The warm springs we were using had a sunstone in the middle of a small, shallow reservoir that we'd swam to. We'd floated in the water for a short time before we'd hauled ourselves onto the rock to get some sun. We were wearing matching academy-issued suits. They were a two-piece fit, but they weren't as revealing as the bikinis I had at home. These were sporty and secure, so there was no chance of nip-slips or snuggies.

"What's that?" I turned my head and peeled open one eye to look at her.

She was resting on her elbows, looking out over the warm springs. It was more of a mini lake surrounded by a beach, waterfalls, and a flat rock to rest on. It was really beautiful and clearly made by fae using two—if not three—elements to achieve.

"I don't think the Star Kicker was glaring at me at all. I think he was always glaring at you."

My pulse raced as I sat up. "What? Why do you say that?"

"I don't want to freak you out. I still think he's a grumpy asshole." She reached her hand out and placed it on mine. "But he's always staring at you."

I felt the blood drain from my face. We were in the sun, so I wondered if I'd paled at her words because my cheeks suddenly felt cooler. "No." I shook my head.

Then, like an idiot, I looked around frantically, knowing he was in our class and hoping she was wrong. She wasn't. Almost immediately, my eyes landed on his. He was resting on a rock with two of his buddies and the same females from the dining hall. They were all laughing and joking around with each other, completely absorbed in their conversation as he glared at me from across the water. The same girl he'd had on his lap in the dining hall was resting against his chest, his arm draped over the front of her, and she ran her fingers up and down his forearm while she laughed with her friends.

I knew I'd stared for several seconds too long when he smirked. It was the tiniest movement, but I saw it. Then, very deliberately, he leaned over and kissed the top of her head with his eyes locked on me.

The pain was severe enough to make my breath catch in my throat. I panicked, and before I knew what had happened, a wall of water shot up between us, cutting off my view and splashing Callie in the process.

"Holy shit! Was that you?" Callie sat up straight and looked up at the watery wall.

I ducked from the splashing droplets as it hovered. "No, but let's go. I don't want to be here when it falls." I grabbed her hand, steering us to the edge of the rock. I hated lying to her, but I didn't want to admit the truth about my magic just yet. My family and I had a plan, and I wasn't meant to reveal more than one element until after I met my next mate.

She giggled as the wall wavered, raining down on us, and her joy was enough to bring me out of my spiral. We dove into the water and swam away from the rock, and toward the beach. When we were halfway back to shore, I let the magic drop. The water crashed into the lake, sending a wave across the spring, but by the time it reached us, we were in the shallows. We stood and walked out of the water before the wake hit. It wasn't big and it wouldn't do any damage, but if we'd still been swimming, it would have dunked our heads.

Callie laughed as we stepped onto the sand, and I turned to find her pointing at Axel and his group.

They were drenched.

None of them seemed to care, apart from Axel. They laughed and looked around, trying to figure out who had conjured the water, but Axel was watching us—or, more specifically, me. His eyes traveled down my wet body in a slow sweep before trailing up again. He swallowed hard, pulling in a deep breath. His fists clenched, and I turned and walked away before his gaze could reach my face.

"I've changed my mind," Callie said, walking next to me. "I don't think he's glaring at you. I know he is. I think he's obsessed with you, too."

I wrinkled my nose. "Fuck him. Don't say that. Gross, Callie."

She tipped her head back and laughed loud enough to draw the attention of others. "You should have seen your face!"

I snorted and bumped her shoulder with my own. "That was mean."

"I was being serious! But you're right—fuck him." Her eyes twinkled mischievously. "We should go out tonight."

I shook my head and opened my mouth to deny her, but she cut me off.

"Come on! It's our first weekend here. We have to go to the welcome bash!"

I was still shaking my head when we entered the locker room.

"Please!" She dragged out the word in her sing-song voice and held her clasped hands under her chin like a child as she begged. "Please, please, please."

I bit back a smile. "I'll think about it."

"Yay!" She clapped her hands and jumped up and down.

"I didn't say yes."

"Not yet!" She winked and scurried off to the showers.

I grabbed my things from my locker and heard the door open with someone's entrance. I had just thrown a towel over my shoulder when the conversation on the other side of the room drew my attention.

"It's weird, Jana. He's always staring at her."

"She's just some dumb first-year. I'm not worried."

"Maybe you should be." The splat of a wet swimsuit hitting the floor echoed around the room. "He watched her the entire time we were sunbathing. If someone hadn't conjured the water, he'd probably still be gawking at her. Just because he's not your mate isn't a pass to be disrespectful to you or your relationship."

She snorted at her friend as another squelch sound hit the floor. "I'll worry when Axe stops fucking me, Meira, and as of right now, I'm still sore from last night."

My heart dropped to the floor as a lump formed in my throat. I darted toward the shower to get away from the rest of the conversation. My pulse pounded through my veins, and I barely got my head under the water before tears streamed down my face. I sucked in a shuddering breath, trying to stay quiet. My shoulders and stomach quaked with the effort. Luckily, the shower stalls were closed off and not one large open space.

It shouldn't have hurt because I truly didn't know him at all. He was a stranger to me in almost every way, yet he still had the power to send me to my knees. Our bond held on by a thread, but what little remained was like a direct line to my heart, and everything he did was still breaking it. I needed it to end. I couldn't endure it any longer. It was only the end of my first week, and I'd cried every day because of him.

I washed my body as I fought to control my tears. When my hair was rinsed and my eyes no longer burned, I used my magic to make myself presentable. I dressed quickly, hastily pulling a comb through my hair before slinging my bag over my shoulder. I found Callie waiting for me outside, leaning against a tree and chatting with a group of males.

"Hey."

"Hey!" she said, grinning. "These guys are from my old prep school. They're the ones that told me about the bash tonight."

The tallest one stuck his hand out. "I'm Jed." He had auburn hair and a leanly muscled body. He was cute, but not my type at all. He pointed to his friends and said, "These two are Brev and Sidric."

Brev was shorter and bulkier than Jed. He had brown hair and brown skin, and pearly white teeth. He was cute, too, but I wasn't attracted to him.

Sidric, on the other hand, was hot as fuck. His gray hair was pulled back in a knot, revealing the shaved sides of his head. Tattoos decorated his scalp, spilling down his neck and disappearing into his black shirt. They reappeared at the edge of his sleeve and ended at his wrists. His eyebrow was pierced and so was his lip. If I had to guess, based on the cocky smile he gave me as I checked him out, he was pierced in other places too.

"What's your name, gorgeous?" Sidric's deep voice rattled through our connected hands.

"Lyra. It's nice to meet you."

He lifted my hand to his lips and flicked his pierced tongue over my skin, following the toe-curling act with a kiss on the wet spot he'd just left. "The pleasure's mine." His breath cooled the skin as he spoke over the dampness he'd left behind.

"Dude, stop tasting my friend." Callie reached up and jerked my hand away from his grasp.

"Only if she wants me to," he said with a wink.

I didn't know what to say, so instead, I blushed.

"Anyway," Jed said, elbowing Sidric in the arm. "Are you and your friend coming with us, Callie?"

She looked to me for an answer, and after what had happened in the locker room, the choice was obvious. "Yes."

Chapter Eight

"So, all three of you are on the Silver Squad?" I asked Jed, Brev, and Sidric.

We'd been chatting at the party for over an hour. It was early evening, and a distant bonfire had left the lingering scent of burned wood and smoke in the air. It was warm, and even though it was still dusk, lightning bugs blinked in and out of view on the horizon.

Callie handed me a cup filled with frothy beer from a keg. Even though I didn't care much for beer, it was cold and refreshing, and I didn't have another option since there wasn't a full bar.

"Yes. They moved a lot of players around this season," Brev said before taking a sip from his cup.

I perked up at that. I still hadn't talked to Puck about why Axel had moved from Silver to Black, but maybe I didn't have to if these guys knew the answer.

"Why is that?"

Brev shrugged. "They gave us some bullshit excuse about balancing the powerful players across both squads, but we know better."

I waited, expecting him to finish his statement, but he lifted his beer and went back to drinking.

A deep chuckle drew my attention to Sidric. "You look confused."

"Well, that wasn't really an answer." I raised a brow and took a sip of my drink.

"Brev struggles with complete sentences."

"Fuck off." He raised his hand and gave him the middle finger.

Sidric leaned forward, ignoring him and explaining further. "Some shit happened last semester, and there was a conflict between several players. We practiced for a few weeks before school started, and the problems hadn't gone away during summer break. So, the players were reassigned to keep the peace. So far, it's worked."

"For you especially," Jed said, fist-bumping Sidric.

"I'm the Star Kicker on the Silver Squad now. I was a second string Star Striker, but... Like I said—it all worked out." Sidric winked.

"Congratulations," I murmured.

"Thank you."

"What problems?" My curiosity took control of my mouth before I could stop it.

"Stupid rumors," Jed said. He had an arm around Callie's shoulders, and he pulled her in close.

Callie perked up at the gossip. "What rumors? I love rumors!"

"I know you do, little rabbit." Jed booped her on the nose before she could bat his hand away.

"Don't call me that! Now, tell me," she demanded, stomping her foot.

"Spring Solstice," Sidric said, and I almost choked on my beer.

Fucking Puck! I knew he'd done something. I wanted to hunt him down and rip him a new asshole, but I seethed quietly instead.

"Oh." Callie rolled her eyes, deflating. "That's dumb."

"Rejecting your fated mate is dumb?" Sidric stared at her like she was insane.

"No, that's not what I meant. The rumor itself is dumb. No one in their right mind would reject their fated mate, so there has to be another reason for the infighting. Besides, they were just rumors, remember? The Spring Court and the Queen released statements."

"That's called a cover-up, sweetheart." Brev lifted his glass as if to cheer the statement.

"Here we go." Callie rolled her eyes and looked at me. "This one has a manifesto of conspiracy theories. Remember that next time you ask for more details."

"All I'm saying is that Puck was at the Spring Revelry, and Axel and his buddy Landor were both in attendance. There was a big-enough fuss about what happened that the Queen herself released a statement, and when we came back to school, Puck refused to play with anyone from the Spring Court."

My mouth practically fell open at the story. "You're not serious."

"Dead serious. Everyone knows how important it is for the Queen to find her Knights. It's what keeps our realms in balance. Puck's my captain, and we've been teammates since my first year, but even if that wasn't the case, I'd still agree with him. If the Night Princess had been there and that had been her…" He shook his head. "We should all be mad, so I understand Puck's anger. If some asshole rejected my baby sister, I'd kick his ass at every opportunity."

"She wasn't there, though," Callie said like she knew what she was talking about. "And the Queen debunked the rumor. Why would she lie?"

"First of all, she could have been there. And if she was, they would have lied about it. That's how it works. Second, if it turns out to be true, imagine the political shitstorm it would cause. The Spring Noble would be disgraced at best, shunned and banished to the wastelands at worst. Who would want to associate with a family like that?"

"Which is why it's obviously a rumor," Callie replied, throwing her arms in the air.

"Then why was Puck so mad?" Brev challenged.

"I don't know. I've never met the guy." Callie put her hands on her hips and scowled. A puzzled look came over her face, and she glanced at me before returning her attention to Brev. "Wait, is Axel the Black Squad's Star Kicker?"

"Duh, Callie. Keep up!"

"Holy shit! He's such an asshole!"

"So, you do know him," Brev said with a nod.

"That doesn't mean the rumor is true."

"It could."

"And that's why the teams were split up," Sidric said with a smirk. He turned to me and whispered, "You're witnessing the exact argument that happened every day for a week when we started preseason practice."

I didn't know what to say. It was all true, but I had no idea that people speculated about it like this. I wondered how many more rumors were circulating about what had happened that night.

"Come on." Sidric grabbed my hand and pulled me past Callie and Brev, who were arguing again.

"Where are we going?"

"To dance," he said, draping his arm around my shoulders.

I was still in shock after hearing the story of Axel's fall from grace, so I didn't question being led into the crowd by a handsome stranger. I was a little buzzed from the beers, so when we started moving together on the dance floor, I let Sidric and the music guide me. The beat pulsed through my body as a sort of euphoria filled the space, and I closed my eyes, ignoring the other couples and throuples bumping and grinding nearby.

Sidric had a firm grip around my waist, his hands resting closer to my ass than my back, while I had entwined my arms around his neck as we danced.

"Let me kiss you," his hot breath whispered against my neck before he pressed his lips into the skin beneath my ear.

I tilted my head to give him better access—and permission. His chest rumbled at my acquiescence, and he pulled me closer as his hand slipped into my hair. The light kisses he trailed over my skin became heavier as he worked his way down my neck and up again.

When he reached my jaw, I tilted my head back, desperate to feel his mouth on mine. He wasn't gentle, and I didn't want him to be. When our lips crashed together, he split my mouth open hungrily, sinking his tongue in to sweep against mine. His piercing was cold, and I moaned at the feel of the metal ball teasing my tongue. I imagined how it would feel against my sex, circling my clit, and I rolled my hips into him. He let out a throaty moan and squeezed my ass, pushing his growing erection into my stomach.

It had been too long since I'd found release with another. Months before I'd been presented, I'd abstained, hoping that I would meet one of my mates. Afterward, I'd been too dejected to even consider the possibility. But after what I'd heard in the locker room?

I was done being the sad little reject.

Sidric nipped at my bottom lip and kissed down the side of my face as both of us panted heavily. "Let's get another drink. Unless you want me to take you to bed now?"

I giggled and pulled back to look at him. He was totally serious, but I liked my options.

"Drinks first. More dancing. Then, you can fuck me and buy me breakfast in the morning."

He growled, crushing his mouth to mine in another searing kiss before pulling away. "Deal," he said, licking my bottom lip.

He liked to lick, and I knew I was going to like his licking.

He spun me around suddenly, and my surprised squeak dissolved into laughter as he pulled me into his arms. Sidric wrapped his arms around me and kissed up the side of my neck as he ground his dick into my ass.

"I need a minute to put this away before we can walk anywhere."

I nodded and bit my lip, failing to hold back my moan. He chuckled, moving his hips away from my curves, and as we danced, I closed my eyes and rested my head against his chest. Each of us tried to maintain our composure, but it was difficult. I wanted to go, but I also didn't want the moment to end.

We swayed together through another song and when it was over, Sidric kissed my temple. "Ready for that drink?"

Nodding, I opened my eyes and found myself caught in Axel's murderous gaze while he danced with Jana several feet away. But as Sidric took my hand, I looked away from Axel and up to him almost seamlessly. Sidric winked, leading me through the crowd to the keg.

"Would you like semi-warm beer or semi-cold beer?" He gestured to the two kegs. One was on the ground next to a block of ice and the other was sitting on top of a block of ice.

I scoffed and shook my head. "Not a single person here with water magic thought to keep the beer cold?"

He laughed as he poured two cups from the semi-cold keg. "Alcohol and brains rarely go together."

We walked through the crowd, making our way back to where we'd left the others. He introduced me to his teammates and friends who stopped him to say hello, which I thought was sweet. Even though we hardly knew each other, he was making an effort to include me, and after each introduction, I felt more comfortable.

"That was some heavy petting out there," Callie whispered in my ear when we found our group. If her slurred words were any indication, she was drunk.

Sidric leaned over and asked, "Didn't you and Jed have a quickie in the forest a little while ago?"

"Shut the fuck up, Sid!" She clicked her tongue and tried to push him away, but the motion sent her stumbling into Jed's waiting arms.

Sidric laughed, draping his arm across my shoulders to pull me into him, where I stayed close to his side as they bantered back and forth like old friends.

It was nice to be a part of their group since I'd had nothing like it before. I had my brothers, and we were like this with each other.

I also had the Day Court siblings. Besides my family, they were the only others in both realms that knew what it was like to be us. Of course, they didn't know my real name or face, but that wasn't off-putting to them since they lived by the same protocol.

It also didn't stop me and the youngest Day Duke from learning our bodies together. He was a year older than me, but we knew about each other since we were little. Then, as we grew older, we'd sneak off together during our biannual summit. Sometimes Garret and I would steal away and meet between those periods, though that had only happened a handful of times.

I tuned in to the conversation as they shared stories about all the trouble they used to cause. Apparently, they'd pranked the headmaster of their old prep school on the first and last day of each year. They'd managed to never get caught, and their stories had me in stitches. For their final prank, they'd dismantled his entire car and encased each piece in hardened honey, stacking the blocks in the auditorium for him to find.

"The school still smells sweet," Jed said with a grin.

I cringed. "For that reason alone, I'm glad I wasn't there. That much honey probably would have killed me."

"You're allergic?" Callie asked, and I nodded in answer. "Good to know! Jeez, that's something your BFF should be warned about!"

"Sorry." I dragged out the word like she did sometimes, which earned me a smile. "What happened after he found his car?"

"No idea. We were gone by then. But we all chipped in and replaced it," Sidric said. "I don't want you to think we're animals. Mr. Gerk had a shiny new set of wheels waiting for him in his spot on the first day of school the following year."

"He deserved it," Callie hiccupped. "We put that poor bastard through hell. Plus, he was so happy." Her drunken smile turned watery at the memory. "He had the biggest grin on his face. It made me want to buy him a new car for each of the years we fucked with him." She hiccupped again as her bottom lip quivered.

She was so sweet.

"All right, little rabbit. Time to get you to bed." Jed pulled her to her feet and wrapped his arms around her waist.

"I'm fine. He was just so happy."

"I know." He grinned down at her as he rubbed her back.

"We should tell him."

The three males groaned. "No, Callie."

"Every time we talk about this when she's drunk, she does this," Brev muttered.

"Shut up, Brev!" Callie ducked under Jed's arm to glare at her friend.

He chuckled and reached out to boop her nose. It seemed to be a habit of theirs, and I assumed it had something to do with the way she wrinkled her nasal bridge. It was probably where the nickname had come from, too. I hadn't seen her twitch her nose as much as she had since meeting them.

"Ugh." She scrubbed her hand over the tip of her face. "You guys are so annoying."

I couldn't help it. I snorted at her. "You're adorable."

Her mouth fell open, and she pointed at me. "Take it back!"

All that did was have me laughing at her. Luckily, she wasn't offended and let out a giggle that was infectious.

"Time to go." Jed turned to leave before coming to a stop, and Callie sucked in a breath. "Did you need something, Axe?" Jed asked, and I stiffened next to Sidric.

Sidric glanced at me, obviously feeling my tension. I hoped he would attribute it to the rumors they'd mentioned earlier.

Axel chuckled, but the sound was cold. "Just came to check in with Sid. See how he likes my spot."

I knew he was talking about Starball, but the double entendre made my heart pound in my chest. Whether he'd meant it like that or not, it's what I heard.

Sidric shook his head, completely ignoring the bait. "Are you ready to go, honey?" he asked, grinning down at me.

"Honey?" I questioned.

"It fits. Plus, you taste sweet, just like the golden nectar."

"Annnd that's my cue." Brev stood and shuffled over to Jed. "The drama with the team has been settled, Axe. Take it up with Coach and the captains."

"Nah. Sidric and I need to chat. Why don't you take *honey* to her room so we can have a word?"

"Let it go, Axe. We've all been drinking." Sidric pulled me with him to stand next to Jed and Callie.

Axel's eyes narrowed on Sidric's arm as it curled around my shoulders. He tracked the length of his forearm before looking directly at me and grinding his teeth.

"No, I don't think I will." He bit out the words, still glaring at me before looking up at Sidric. "Send your plaything back to her room so we can talk."

"Don't talk about her, and don't fucking disrespect my girl."

"She's not yours!" Axel stepped forward as he yelled. "She's just some female you met tonight. Stop hiding behind her."

Brev moved between us, blocking our view of each other. "Take the ladies back to their rooms. I'll stay with Axe and work this out."

"Works for me," Jed said, turning Callie so they could walk away.

"Yep," Sidric agreed.

"You think you're strong enough to stop me from getting what I want?" Axel snarled at Brev.

"Maybe, maybe not," Brev replied. "But I know I'm sober, and I'm banking on you not being stupid enough to start a fight here with all these witnesses. You'd really risk getting yourself kicked off the team because of a bruised ego?"

"Fuck you," Axel hissed.

Sidric steered me away from the fight, and their voices faded as we ambled toward my dorm. I felt uneasy about leaving Brev to deal with Axel. Axel was a large, powerful male, and I knew his shifted form would be formidable. As much as it pained me to admit it, his strength and abilities would be equal to my own. It's why we'd been chosen for each other, and just because he'd thrown it away didn't mean he'd lost his vitality. But Sidric and Jed reassured me that Brev could handle the situation, and since I had no choice, I had to believe them.

Chapter Nine

Sidric's hard body was wrapped around me when I woke the next morning. I smiled at the pleasant ache between my thighs, and as I shifted around, he pulled me closer and pushed his dick against my ass.

"I promised you breakfast, but if you don't stop wiggling around, I'll eat you instead." Sidric's sleepy voice vibrated in his chest against my back.

I didn't know if I could handle another round with his frenum ladder without healing myself first, but I was willing to find out. I pushed back into him again. The only warning I got was the faint sound of his lips spreading into a smile and the silent chuff of his breath.

He rolled me onto my stomach, split my legs open, and pushed his cock inside me. My moans were punctuated by the sound of the bed cracking against the wall. He kneeled behind me with one hand on my hip and the other on my headboard as he hammered into me.

I was still sensitive from the night before, so it didn't take more than a few minutes before I was clenching around him and crying my release into my pillow. He picked up his pace and followed suit before collapsing next to me.

I sighed and turned to look at him. "Good morning."

His features were still sleep-rumpled, but there was a satisfied look on his face I was sure he'd wear all day long. I knew I would.

"Morning." He reached over and brushed the hair out of my eyes. Then, he closed the distance between us and kissed me thoroughly.

We showered quickly, and as I combed my hair and applied light makeup, he put on his clothes from the night before. They were still clean, and he whisked away the lingering scent of smoke with his wind magic.

It wasn't early when we left my room, but by the looks of the students around campus, we were off to a better start than most. I noticed a lot of messy buns and sweatpants, and plates of dining hall food.

When we came to the walkway that headed toward the cafeteria, I followed the aroma of food, but Sidric tugged on my shirt and brought me back against him.

"Where are you going?"

"To breakfast," I said, confused.

He shook his head. "Did you really think I was going to take you to the school commons for a free breakfast?"

I looked over my shoulder toward where the smell of pancakes was coming from, then back up to him. "Yes?"

"I'm wounded." He slid his arm around my shoulders and turned us away from the smell of sausages. "I know we just met yesterday, honey, but when I tell you I'm taking you out to eat, you can assume it's not anywhere on campus."

Araphel Academy was in the Darkport district of the Luna Realm, and since it was a college town, there were tons of options. Coffee shops, bars, and bistros dotted every corner, and the streets were filled with shops and boutiques. There were even some dining options that didn't comprise of mostly fried foods.

Sidric took me to a little café that served breakfast all day. We each ordered a large cup of coffee and their hangover special, which was what it was called and was featured at the top of the menu. It came with eggs benedict with avocado and tomato, veggie bacon and sausage, hash browns, fruit, and toast. Plus, your choice of a side of pancakes, biscuits and country gravy, or beans on toast.

There was no way on Gaia's green earth that I could eat everything, but I ordered it anyway, adding a side of pancakes since I'd been craving them. Sidric added a side of biscuits and gravy to his order, promising that whatever I didn't finish, he'd dutifully take.

We chatted through our first cup of coffee and dug into our food when it arrived. I barely ate half before I felt like I was going to explode out of my romper. Meanwhile, Sidric had nearly devoured his entire plate and was already helping himself to mine.

While he finished the rest of my food, I told him about myself. The thing about being completely unknown was that I could tell him about me because no one knew anything to compare it to. So, I told him about my pets I had growing up and my annoying brothers. It wasn't uncommon to have a family the size of mine, so I felt comfortable sharing stories about my siblings. I only mentioned three of my brothers since anything I said about Puck could have clued him in by the comparison. Puck had a big personality and wasn't shy about sharing his life, so nothing was safe for me to discuss. I told him about my classes, hobbies, and the books I was reading.

When he finished eating, he returned my answers with his own. He told me he was studying infrastructure and renewable energy. Most of the Faery Realms were powered by magic, but that required someone to cast into it or draw directly from the earth, so there had been a big push to harness natural energy. He had two sisters who were both fully mated, and though he wasn't from a noble family, his great-great-grandfather had been a Day Noble from the Autumn Court, which was really interesting.

We finished breakfast and took our third cup of coffee to go. Sidric laced his fingers with mine as we strolled down the side streets back to campus and window-peaked at some shops. I didn't have any need for anything, so even though he'd offered to go inside with me, I didn't take him up on it.

When we stepped onto school grounds, we were met with the same sort of phlegmatic energy, though there were a lot more students now that had emerged from their rooms. Groups of students were sprawled across the grass, resting under trees, and the picnic tables were full as the low hum of conversation filled the air.

We debated joining the crowd for a quick nap in the grass, but Sidric spotted something over my shoulder and frowned.

"Fucking hell, honey. Maybe you should go to your room?" His brow furrowed as he looked down at me. "I don't know what his problem is, but you don't need to be part of it."

I had known who he was talking about long before the jerk in question made his presence known.

"Okay," I replied, all too willing to take the out he was giving me. I had zero desire to deal with Axel and his attitude, especially after such a wonderful morning with Sidric. "Thanks for breakfast."

He bent down to kiss me. "Thanks for last night ... and this morning." His words weren't quiet, but his breath was a whisper against my lips. He crushed his mouth to mine, pulling a moan from my throat.

"Knock it the fuck off," Axel growled from somewhere behind me.

I ignored him, and so did Sidric.

"I'll message you later, honey."

I blushed and gave him an answering smile since I couldn't seem to find my voice. He released me and I turned to walk away, stepping around Axel in the process. I could feel his glare on my face, but I refused to look at him as I passed.

"Are you fucking serious?" His words were low and aimed at me, but I didn't acknowledge him.

How could I? We weren't supposed to know each other. Unless he wanted to out himself as the idiot who had rejected his fated mate, he had to keep his mouth shut—and I knew he would because his family had taken the first steps in covering it up.

If he was angry at our situation, he only had himself to blame.

Chapter Ten

Sidric and I messaged each other over the weekend while I worked ahead on my course assignments. Callie studied with me in my room for part of the next day, and after we had lunch together, we went to her room. She showed me her dragon fruit mushroom tree, which was exactly like it sounded but totally unexpected. The waist-high edible mushroom had the skin and coloring of dragon fruit, but under its cap, tiny dragon fruits and mini versions of the plant dangled from the fibers. They were sweet like the fruit but chewy like a mushroom, and it was the weirdest thing I'd ever eaten. I loved it.

Afterward, she told me about her experiments with hybridizing plants and herbs to create new, more effective treatments. She was especially interested in my allergy to honey.

"I hope you don't mind, but I thought I'd experiment with known treatments and honey itself to see if I can help. I don't have any delusions that I can cure you of the allergy. At least not yet," she said, winking at me. It was then that I knew her passion wasn't solely based on her parents' desire for her to take over the family business. She was really interested in what she was doing. Her selfless desire to study my allergy after just hearing about it was more than just a duty for her—it was a passion. "But I think I might be able to come up with a stronger treatment, given time."

"That's incredible, Callie. I don't know what to say."

"Say you'll help? It'll make it much easier if I have your input."

"I'll tell you anything you wish to know, but I can't let you experiment on me."

She wrinkled her brow. "I would never put you in danger."

"You misunderstand. I want to help, Callie, but I'm deathly allergic. Normally, that rule only applies to a bee sting, but it's both for me." Her eyes widened as I explained. "When I was very young, my brothers and I were playing in a flower field and I was swarmed by a nest. There was no way to determine how many times I'd been stung. I almost didn't survive. I was in intensive care for a week. My family provided the best healers, but I was so young and fragile that even their magic wasn't enough. Obviously, my body rallied, but if honey even touches my skin, it could send me into anaphylaxis. I break out in hives, my temperature rises, and my skin feels like it's on fire. Contact with honey takes a little bit longer to affect me, but it still does. I'm not a scientist, but I think my allergy has something to do with bee venom, and that's what made me allergic to both. A bee sting causes a near-instantaneous reaction."

"Oh my goddess, Lyra! That's severe." She placed her hand on my shoulder. "I'm glad you told me. You should be more open about it if it's that dangerous."

I shrugged. "I avoid it. My earrings are charmed to repel bees from flying around me. If I know honey is being served at meals, I won't eat any of the food out of fear of cross-contamination, and I'm diligent about checking ingredients. An allergic reaction isn't likely."

"But what if someone snuck it into your food or drink?"

"I always use a detection spell before I eat or drink. You may not have noticed because it's become second nature to me, but before I consume anything—"

"You wave your hand over it!" She almost cheered like this was a quiz and she'd gotten the answer right. "I did notice! I just thought it was a silly tic or something. So, no experimenting directly on you, but I wonder..." She put her finger to her mouth as a faraway look came over her face. "Jed is studying genetics, and he does a lot with blood and skin samples. I wonder if I could test samples from you? I could get some equipment from him, or maybe I could use his lab. Would you give me blood? Or I could scrape cells from your mouth? Or both, actually—that would be better."

The more she talked, the more my mouth went slack with surprise. She was serious about this.

"It wouldn't hurt, and I'd only need a little each time I wanted to test something. You'd never be in danger," she assured me, misunderstanding my silence.

"I'll help you, Callie. I'm just shocked you'd go to such lengths for me."

She waved her hand in the air. "Are you kidding? I'd do it because you're my friend, but don't get me wrong—this is a dream experiment! I can use my research and findings for almost all my classes, and if I'm successful—which I will be—we'll both benefit from my work. I bet Jed will take an active interest, too, since he can use the research as well. Lyra, you've actually given me a gift with your allergy."

"If you can help me at all, it will be you who has given me a gift, Callie," I said, pulling her into my arms for a hug. I knew I'd likely never be able to enjoy honey, but it would be nothing short of a miracle to lessen the symptoms or prevent my death if I encountered it.

She started rambling about experiments and ideas as they came to her, all of which made no sense to me, but I listened anyway. She didn't want samples from me right then, not until she had a working theory to test and equipment to use.

We stayed in her room until dinner, and when we went to the dining hall, it was busier than it had been all weekend. Sidric, Jed, and Brev joined us, and even though I'd just met them, it all felt very familiar and casual. There wasn't any awkwardness either, which I was thankful for since the entire table knew Sidric and I had slept together. Of course, our relationship wasn't serious. Fae interludes rarely were. We all knew we could meet our mates at any time, so casual was the standard.

The following morning, my stomach twisted with nerves before my Economics class. Axel was in it, and it would be the first time I'd seen him since he'd pulled me into that room and after I'd seen him at the bonfire. I didn't know what Axel and Sidric had talked about after I'd left them in the courtyard, but I didn't think Axel planned to leave me alone.

As I walked into the classroom, I pulled my shoulders back and put on a brave face. I wasn't as early as last week, but I found Professor Warrock resting against his desk again, watching students enter the room. He smiled at me and gave me a nod as I found my seat.

Axel was already at his desk. His leg was bouncing up and down, and his arms were crossed over his chest. He was agitated, but he kept his eyes forward and didn't acknowledge me in any way.

Professor Warrock went right into his lecture. I'd already worked ahead, but I took notes on his perspective and insight anyway. It was always good to have other views, and even though the fundamentals didn't change, people's interpretations of them and how they applied them would.

Our class periods were two-hour time blocks, and when he'd finished his instruction, there was just under an hour left. As soon as he told everyone to begin the assignment, I pulled up my finished work and sent it in electronically. I thought nothing of it and began reading ahead. I'd completed several assignments, so I opened my textbook and picked up where I'd left off.

A shadow darkened my desk, and I looked up to find Professor Warrock towering over me, holding his tablet with a quizzical look on his face.

"You worked ahead?"

"I did. Was I not supposed to?"

His lips twitched. "No, Ms. Bruadar, it's perfectly acceptable. Not typical, but there are no rules against working ahead." Then, to my surprise, he took the seat next to me.

I watched as he began grading my assignment. He smirked, knowing I was staring at him. It was odd, and I didn't know what to do, so I went back to reading and taking notes.

Before I knew it, the bell rang for us to leave. I quickly finished what I was jotting down and stuffed my tablet in my bag. When I went to stand, I realized Professor Warrock was watching me, drumming his fingers on the table.

The dining hall was quiet, and we ate quickly before splitting off to our respective classes. I still had fifteen minutes until class started, but I went inside anyway to claim a seat at the back. I wasn't expecting the professor to be there, though.

He was writing on the board and turned around at the sound of the door.

"Pardon me, is it all right that I'm early?" I stopped before fully entering.

"Of course." He smiled and turned to face me.

He was handsome and tall with a trim figure. His dark brown hair was styled short and feather-combed to the side, and his clean-shaven face held a kind smile and a youthful appearance. I don't know why I thought he'd be old, but if I had to guess, he wasn't a day over twenty-five. Though, that didn't mean anything. I had great-grandparents that looked the same age as my parents.

He waved me down to the front as he leaned against his desk. Once there, he turned his upper body toward me and grabbed a clipboard. "What's your name?"

The door opened as a group of students came into the room. Professor Warrock flicked his eyes up to them but quickly returned his gaze to the paper in front of him.

"Lyra Bruadar." I gave him my real first name, which was a closely guarded secret that had never been released to the public. Along with my fake last name that had been won by drawing it out of a hat. My real last name was on every building here. Araphel. It was the Night Queen's institution, after all.

He looked up and gave me a little smirk. "Dream?"

I blushed, nodding. "It's silly." I shrugged.

"I think it's fitting."

I flicked my eyes up to him. Was he ... flirting with me? Was that allowed? I didn't know.

"It's nice to meet you, Lyra. Have a seat wherever you'd like." He gave me a lazy smile that made my belly flip. He wasn't my mate. If he had been, we both would have known immediately. But he was still attractive, and since I didn't have any attachments...

"Have you finished all the assignments up to lesson six?"

Pulling the strap of my bag over my head and settling the weight on my shoulder, I answered, "I have. I'm not entirely confident with my answers for lesson five, though."

"The lecture will clear up any confusion." He stood and swiped his finger over his tablet. Mine pinged in my bag, letting me know I'd received something from him. It was likely my graded work. "But based on the perfect score you just earned, I can't imagine you've struggled too much with the work. I'm eager to see how you do this year, Ms. Bruadar." He nodded and returned to his desk.

I blushed as I hurried out of the classroom. I didn't exactly know how to respond. I took pride in my work, but I was also aware of the privilege that had been afforded to me thanks to my station. I had to work hard. I was just lucky I enjoyed learning as much as I did and wanted to succeed more than my duty required. It would be rather embarrassing and not very comforting for my people if the future queen failed her coursework. That wouldn't exactly instill trust in one's ability to guide the realm.

"We need to talk." Axel appeared next to me, and before I knew it, he was steering me into the same room he'd pulled me into last week. The only difference was that he pushed me with his hand on my back instead of jerking me around by my arms. He also stood in front of the door after closing it.

"I disagree. We have nothing to talk about," I argued, but he crossed his arms over his chest and planted his feet.

"We do."

I shook my head. "We don't. Anything I would have been interested in hearing you say became irrelevant on Spring Solstice. Any affiliation between us ended before it began. You got what you wanted. Now, I must insist you leave me alone."

"Are you fucking him?"

"Excuse me?"

"Sidric. Are you fucking him?" The words were clipped as he spoke.

"That's none of your business. Nothing I do is any of your business. Now, let me pass." I stepped toward the door, not expecting him to move but hoping he would.

"Stop seeing him and stop flirting with the fucking teacher, Lyra," he ordered. "I told you to leave. Why don't you just fucking go?"

I shook my head in disbelief. "How dare you?"

"How dare I?" he yelled. "You've been here a week, and you're already fucking one of my teammates. You've got the professor drooling all over you, and I'm half convinced you've given your little girlfriend a taste too."

My mouth fell open. "Are you kidding me?"

"It's bad enough that you're here, but this is bullshit."

I sighed and folded my hands together in front of me. I didn't want to feel compassion for him, but it was inevitable. The bond wasn't fully severed, so he was forced to feel the remnants of the rejection too. And while it had been his decision, I knew from personal experience how uncomfortable it was to feel any kind of way about someone you didn't want to.

"Axel," I said, lowering my voice so he wouldn't think I was berating him. A sound I couldn't place rumbled in his throat, and his hands balled into fists. "Whatever this is about will go away once you leave me alone. You confronting me isn't helping. I don't owe you anything. I don't owe you an explanation or my time. I don't know you. You are a stranger, and this is incredibly inappropriate."

"Inappropriate? This is inappropriate, but you fucking someone isn't?"

"No. Why would it be?"

"Why would it be? Are you fucking kidding me right now, Lyra? You know why!"

"It shouldn't matter. Aren't you fucking Jana?"

He jerked back, scoffing. "What?"

"What is this about? Why are you doing this?"

"I want you to leave."

"I already told you I'm not leaving," I said, shaking my head.

"I want you to leave this school, Lyra."

"I'm not going anywhere. You have no right to ask me that or anything else."

"You can't be here. I can't have you here." His voice grew louder.

"It's not up to you. I'm. Not. Leaving."

"Fuck!" He spun on his heel and punched the wall before facing me and wrapping his hands around my biceps. "Don't you get it? I can't have you here. I can't see you every day! I didn't want..." He stuttered, hesitating as his chest heaved. "I don't want you here."

"Well, that's too bad." I pushed him away, and he let me. "This is a consequence of the choice you made for both of us. You're making it worse! You didn't want this. Let the remnants of our bond fade. Stop harassing me and move on, Axel."

"Don't force my hand. I haven't made this difficult for you yet, but I will."

I let out a huff. "You are unbelievable. You really are the most selfish person in all the realms."

"You don't know shit about me, little nightmare. You're nothing. You were nothing when I met you, and you'll be nothing when I get everything I want. Remember that," he spit the words at me, reaching for the door handle.

"No," I boomed. "You remember this, Axel. I want you to remember everything you've ever said to me from the moment we met because it will be the only thing that keeps you warm at night. You will never get what you broke to have. You are a selfish, greedy, power-hungry male who doesn't deserve the blessing that was bestowed upon you. I am not what you want or what you think you deserve—and I wholeheartedly agree. But I promise you will never get what you seek."

Chapter Eleven

I left a seething Axel behind, but he didn't try to stop me as I stormed into the hall. He didn't corner me or attempt to speak to me for the rest of the week either, and I figuratively kept my fingers crossed that him pulling me into that room to accost me would be the last.

Campus was abuzz with excitement at the start of the weekend. It was the opening game of the season, and we were hosting Cascadia Academy's Starball team, the Sharks. The Winter Court students were staying in the guest dorms, and they were mingling in the courtyard as I made my way to my room.

Callie and I had plans to meet up with the guys for dinner in town. The game was scheduled for early afternoon the following day, so there would be no drinking or partying for them.

There were a bunch of parties and a ton of school spirit, though, so I picked out a shirt with the team logo on the front and paired it with shorts and some sandals. I pulled my hair up into a messy bun, shoved my wallet into my back pocket and my cell in the other, and went to Callie's room.

"Where'd you get that shirt?" she squealed when she opened the door.

It was a vintage t-shirt from when my mom was a student. She'd had it spelled so it wouldn't fade, and before I left, she'd packed it for me with some of the other shirts and hats that I'd collected over the years.

"It was my mom's," I told her as I did a little spin so she could see the back.

It was black with silver lettering. Our mascot was a shadow, which was the fae form all the Night Queens and Princesses could take. Becoming one with the dark was badass, and even though the mascot itself was just a wispy, sparkly swirl of smoke, everyone knew what it represented.

"It's so rad! It's a Black Squad shirt, though. Hopefully the asshole doesn't say something if he sees you wearing it."

"He's not the only one on the Black Squad. It represents our school, and he can kiss my ass." I shrugged and gave her a big, toothy grin.

When she finished her makeup, we hurried down to meet the guys.

Sidric sauntered over when he saw us. "Nice shirt, honey. I'm going to enjoy taking it off later," he whispered in my ear after pulling me into his chest.

I giggled and pressed a kiss to his lips.

"Are we ready?" he asked the others after we separated. Before they could answer, he bent down and flipped me over his shoulder. "All right then, let's go!" He smacked my ass, and I squealed.

Sidric ignored my protests and kept hold of me as he walked across campus. Any time we crossed paths with someone he knew, they shouted encouragement so he gripped me tighter.

When we got to the gate, he pulled me across the front of him and held me in his arms while the blood settled back down into my body. I wasn't upset with him—he was excited like everyone else, and the big grin on his face had me smiling in return.

"Don't wear yourself out. You have a big day tomorrow," I said, wiggling in his hold.

He snorted as he released me. "If that was your way of saying you're too heavy for me to carry around all night, I have news for you, honey. I'm twice your size, and you barely weigh a thing."

I rolled my eyes and tried to protest, but he shut me up with a kiss.

"We get it. You like each other. Let's go," Brev grumbled as he walked past. Sidric and I chuckled, splitting apart to follow him.

"He's just mad he isn't getting lucky tonight," Jed teased as he kissed Callie on the head.

"Fuck off," Brev said over his shoulder, but I saw the smirk on his face before he turned back around.

We ended up at a fire-grilled pizza place that was packed with students from both academies. Even with the crowd, there were tons of seats inside and out. We looked for a spot inside where it was a little cooler, but Sidric shook his head.

"Nope," Sidric told the host when he pointed to a table near the front. "We want to sit outside. There aren't any assholes out there."

Confused, we looked at the table next to the one the host wanted to seat us at. Sitting there were Axel, Jana, and their friends.

Axel must have heard what Sidric said because he turned to look in our direction at the same time we saw him.

"Yeah, fuck that. Outside it is," Jed said. "Lead the way, good sir," he told the host.

We had to walk by their table to get outside, but I'd take that over having to sit near them any day of the week.

"Oh look, it's the stolen valor crew and their tramp stamps," Jana snarked as we walked past.

I was all for ignoring her stupid taunt, but the guys weren't having it.

"Didn't you fuck the whole Sharks team last year?" Brev wondered out loud.

"Nah, that was Meira," Sidric added. "You're thinking of the championship game last year when she entertained the guest dorm and all of the Day Court players."

"That's right," Brev snapped his fingers. "That was after what's his name got *axed* for being a super douche."

I groaned, and when we were outside, I grumbled, "You guys are just going to encourage them."

"Fuck that entire table," Callie added.

"Not literally, though, babe." Jed tickled her.

"Ew, gross," she whined, wrinkling her nose.

Luckily, Axel's table didn't follow us to continue their harassment, and whatever they said behind our backs as we walked away fell on deaf ears.

We enjoyed our dinner and conversation, and I only felt eyes on me for part of the time there. We laughed as Jana and Meira flipped us off as they walked by on their way back to campus.

After dinner, we didn't linger since the guys all had to be up early. Back at our dorm, Brev said goodnight as Jed and Sidric followed us upstairs. Jed and Sidric were talking strategy, so when the elevator door opened on Callie's floor, the four of us stepped out and walked her and Jed to her room. Callie and I coordinated our outfits for the game, and we made plans to meet up for breakfast. When they finished their conversation, Sidric and I walked down the hallway, planning to take the stairs up to my floor.

Jana's whining drew our attention. She was standing in her doorway, pulling on his shirt to get him to come inside. "Please, Axie, you haven't stayed in weeks. I want you."

"I said no," he snapped.

"Why? Just stay. I promise it'll be worth it."

Sidric chuckled in my ear as we walked by. "Well, that's embarrassing."

I tried to ignore Axel and Jana's conversation, but Sidric's comment made Axel aware of us when he hadn't been before.

"On second thought, I think I will stay with you tonight," he said.

I didn't look at either of them. I kept my head tucked into Sidric's chest. But there was a surprised gasp from Jana before a loud bang as her door slammed shut.

"That doesn't sound like a fun time," Sidric murmured, but I kept quiet.

I knew what I was heading up to my room to do with Sidric, but I still didn't want to think about what Axel was doing in that room with Jana.

Chapter Twelve

We were up by one, but the Sharks were on offense and tensions were high. The air crackled with magic as the players moved up and down the field, gaining and losing ground. The Sharks were trying to get the ball to their Star Kicker to score and tie the game while our Guards and Strikers tried to hold them off and dispel their magic.

The game was simple. Four Forward Elementals cast out their magic to the Vesseler, who maintained it with a spell in the form of a ball. Together, they had to work to get the ball in position so the Star Kicker could punt it past the defending team's Star Striker and into the goal. All while fighting off magical and physical attacks from the Center Guard, Tackle Guards, and Defense Stoppers.

The Sharks' Vesseler took a hit to the back from our Center Guard, who was the only player allowed to attack the Vesseler. His Forward Elementals tried to focus as he fought off the attack, but our Tackle Guards went after them at the same time. In a panic, their Star Kicker took a chance as the clock ran out. He kicked the ball, sending it toward Axel—the Black Squad's Star Striker—but Axel dove in front of it and blocked the goal.

A buzzer blared through the arena, and the crowd went wild.

"The Shadows win the game," the announcer shouted, and his voice echoed over the cheers as loud music was pumped into the stadium.

"That was awesome!" I yelled, jumping up and down with Callie, who was just as happy. We hugged each other excitedly before turning back to our team to cheer them on.

I caught sight of my brother, who was laughing and celebrating with the teams. He beamed at me for a second before looking away. I'd congratulate him later. I was so freaking proud of him. Winning the opening game of his master year was a great start to the perfect season he was aiming for.

The cheerleaders swarmed the field and flung themselves into the fray. Jana launched herself at Axel, nearly taking him to the ground. He had to have been looking at something else when she'd thrown herself at him, but when he saw I was watching, he wrapped his arms around her as her legs circled his waist. I looked away after that. Whatever happened next was none of my business, and I didn't want to see it.

I waved at Jed, who caught sight of me and Callie, then Brev, and finally Sidric. I laughed when he winked and blew me a kiss. Then the Star Kicker on the other team approached him, pulling his attention away from the stands. Even though the Sharks had lost, we were all still part of the larger Night Kingdom Team, so they congratulated our players and planned to stay for the post-game parties and celebrations. It was good to have that type of camaraderie. When the season wrapped up, one of our courts would represent us at the Dusk to Dawn Championship to see who would carry the title and hold the trophy for the year.

The crowd dispersed, and Callie and I grabbed some tailgate food on the quad while the teams did their post-game rituals. We mingled and shared our excitement with other students before eventually finding our way to the after-party.

"There's our personal cheer squad," Jed hollered over the crowd when he saw us. He stood with Sidric and Brev, surrounded by a horde of teammates. Members of both squads were in attendance, including the captains—my brother and his mate, Roko.

When we got close enough, Jed picked Callie up and practically tossed her in the air with excitement.

"Jed!" she screamed. "Stop! It! Now!" Each word came out in a wail as she fell into his arms from his repeated throwing her in the air.

"Congratulations!" I hugged Brev and sidled up to Sidric, who gathered me in his arms. "That was a great game," I said against his lips.

"Fuck yeah, it was." He kissed me again, then set me down. "Have you met our captains?" He held out his hand in introduction.

It was a bit odd being introduced to my brother, but it was something we'd gone over at home, so we fell into our practiced routine.

"Nice to meet you." I shook his hand.

He laughed, which I'd smack him for later, but he played along.

"Nice to meet you too. It's Honey, right?" he asked with a glint in his eye.

My mouth dropped open before I could catch it, and Sidric cackled next to me. "Oh fuck, that's good."

I elbowed him playfully before correcting my antagonizing brother. "No, that's just what this dork calls me. My name is Lyra."

"Oh shit, my bad. Nice to meet you, Lyra." Puck grinned at me. Then his features changed a little as he reached for his mate, Roko. "This is Roko, the Black Squad's captain and my mate."

I wanted to pull him in for a hug and tell him how excited I was to finally meet him, but I couldn't. It was hard to contain myself, but I managed.

"It's so nice to meet you," I told him, trying not to get misty-eyed.

"It's a pleasure to meet you too." He nodded amicably, totally unaware of how important our introduction was to both Puck and me. It was at times like this that the rule of my identity being kept hidden was really unfair.

They fell into easy conversation, with Callie and me mostly listening while they went over the game. We grabbed drinks and gathered around a small fire. The conversation turned to other topics, but they always circled back to the game, time and time again.

Our group grew, then diminished. Brev had one of the cheerleaders on his lap when Jed pulled Callie up to dance, then he and the female joined them on the dance floor.

"Do you want another drink?" Sidric asked me.

"Sure." I held out my cup.

Roko stood, grabbing Puck's empty glass. "I'll go with you. Be right back."

As the two of them went to the kegs, Puck got up and sat down next to me.

"What are you doing?" I grumbled, pretending to pick something from my shoe.

"It's fine. We are all friends at the party. Chill." He bumped my shoulder. "So, you and Sid, huh? How'd that happen?"

I wrinkled my nose. "You really want to talk about that with me?"

He pulled his head back with a sour look on his face. "Yeah, no. Tell me about your classes instead."

I raised my brows at him. "No way. Tell me why you had the players on both teams mixed up?"

His eyes widened, and he shook his head. His voice was quiet but intense when he said, "You know why. I'm not going to play with that piece of shit, Lyra."

"Puck..."

"I know. I tried, okay? I couldn't do it. Thankfully, I wasn't the only one who had a problem with him. No one knows the truth, but the rumors were enough."

"And because Roko's your mate, he took one for the team."

"Literally." He smiled. "He's pretty fucking great. I wish you could meet him officially."

"Me too." I reached out and squeezed his hand quickly before dropping it.

"Are Jana and her friends a problem?" he asked.

"It's nothing I can't handle. She's just mouthy and taking Axel's lead, but she hasn't done anything worth mentioning. She's just a bitch."

He snorted.

"Who's a bitch?" Roko asked as he handed Puck his drink, taking a seat next to his mate.

"Jana," Puck supplied helpfully.

I glared at my brother. "I know she's your cheerleader. We're just not friends."

"No, I agree. She's a bitch, cheerleader or not. She tried to get on Puck's dick for months, even after she knew we were mates. Uncouth twat," Roko grumbled, taking a long sip of his beer.

Puck leaned over and kissed Roko on the head. "I wouldn't touch her with Axel's dick, let alone mine." He chuckled, then caught himself and flicked his eyes to me.

I gave him the tiniest shake before laughing at his joke.

"Jana's been a problem for Lyra," Sidric added. "But I'm afraid that has more to do with me than anything you did, honey." He lifted my hand and kissed the back. "Axel's been a noble prick since I took his spot on the team, and Lyra's getting the runoff, it would seem."

It was sweet of him to say and only partially off the mark. It was probably both of us, but we couldn't tell him that.

"He'll get over it." Roko shrugged. "I don't know why he's got such a problem with being on Black. He's a better Star Striker than he was a Star Kicker, anyway. The Black Squad is where he will most likely rank. He wasn't even close on Silver."

I agreed. He had only been moved from offense to defense, but his position and its importance remained the same. Roko was right about Axel being a great Star Striker. Not that I was watching him closely or paying attention to him throughout the entire game.

"Fucking A right," Puck agreed. "His ego is bruised, but if he'd pull his head out of his ass, he'd see he's a better fit for Black."

"Who's that?" Malor, the Black squad's Waterback, asked. He sat down next to Puck, who quickly filled him in on what we were talking about.

Some other team members came over, and the group returned to recapping the game. Jed, Callie, Brev, and the cheerleader joined us shortly after that, and there was soon a small crowd around the fire.

"When their Center Guard froze the ground under you and shoved you with that gust of wind, I thought it was over right then and there," Brev told Puck.

"Fuck, me too. That was a slick-ass move." Puck leaned forward and fist-bumped the Sharks' Center Guard.

The guy gave him a mischievous grin and returned the gesture. "Don't be stealing my tricks now, Night Duke."

Puck snorted. "You showed your hand. You bet your ass we'll be stealing that move, and we'll use it at the championship this year."

The surrounding group cheered.

"I still can't believe you didn't fall on your ass." Malor chuckled.

"I'm quick like lightning," Puck said, puffing out his chest as Roko rolled his eyes.

"You're a damn good Vesseler is what you are," I told him, beaming. "Your hold on the form spell only slipped for a second before you had it back. It was amazing."

"Aw, shucks." He batted his hand at me. "You're making me blush, honey." The group laughed as he batted his eyelashes.

"What? The teacher and the Star Kicker aren't enough for you? You want the captain too?" Axel's sneering voice interrupted the fun—literally. Everyone's laughter died off as they looked around in confusion.

I looked up at him, and the smile fell from my face. "You know he's mated, right?" Axel slurred. "Unless you're aiming to be the Night Duke's mistress? You're doing a good job of getting around."

Puck was up and out of his chair in a flash, throwing his fist in Axel's face before anyone could stop him. All hell broke loose, and it was entirely aimed at Axel.

Callie grabbed my hand as Sidric took my chin between his fingers and turned my face to look at him. "Hey, he's a fucking asshole. Ignore him. No one believes a thing he has to say."

I nodded, but I couldn't help the tears gathering in my eyes. Between the excitement of the game, spending time with my brother, and meeting his mate for the first time, plus the alcohol, I was emotional.

"I'm ready to leave."

Sidric nodded and kissed my forehead. "I'll take you back to your room."

"I'm coming too. I've had enough asshole air for one night." Callie squeezed my hand.

Jed walked with us, and I leaned into Sidric's side as we made our way back to my dorm. Although the night had ended on a bitter note, I felt grateful to have such wonderful friends, and I silently thanked the moon for bringing them into my life.

Chapter Thirteen

After Axel's very public comment, Jana, Meira, and their friend, Lacy, took it as an open invitation to taunt me at every given opportunity. They'd previously called me names, but now they weren't holding back.

"Excellent work, Lyra," Professor Warrock said after posting the mid-term grades.

The school posted the grades of its top students for everyone to see. The students were ranked in the top five of each class, the top one hundred for each term, and an overall top one-hundred rank for the school. Cells pinged throughout the room as each student received the mid-term assessment bracket. I pulled out my phone and checked the rankings, shocked to see I'd made it to the top five in my grade and the top ten in the school. I knew I was doing well, but the ranking surprised me.

"I guess it pays to fuck the teacher," Lacy quipped.

My head snapped up to find Professor Warrock glowering at the female in the back of the class. The other students shuffled around and mumbled, but no one agreed with her or added to her comment. No one disagreed or argued with her either. Aside from Axel, who snorted, which might as well have been his seal of approval.

"If you believe fucking a teacher equates to good grades, Ms. Ledark, I wonder why you've never propositioned me to elevate your status?" Professor Warrock leaned against his desk and crossed his arms. "You are at the bottom of my class, after all."

The room erupted with laughter. I packed my bag, keeping my eyes down. I knew she was implying that my grades could have only been earned through sexual favors, but she hadn't called me out by name, so I pretended to not take offense to it.

She sucked in a breath. "So, you admit it?" Her voice was high and tight. She was likely embarrassed for being called out about her ranking but unwilling to let the attention stay on her.

"This is why you didn't rank, Ms. Ledark. Your deduction skills are lacking, and you jump to conclusions without considering the facts. No, I don't fuck my students for higher grades. The answer to your next question is also no. I will not fuck you to raise your mark, Ms. Ledark."

She screeched as the other student howled at her expense. "I don't want to fuck you!"

"The feeling is more than mutual," he said as the bell rang.

"I'm reporting you to the dean!"

"For what? Refuting your sexual advances?" he asked her incredulously, and I bit back a smirk. "Perhaps I should report you, Ms. Ledark. What is your first name again? I want to make sure I spell it right on the form." He smiled as she screamed and hurried out of the room. "See you next week," he called after her.

We exchanged a knowing glance as I moved past, neither of us saying anything to the other. In the hall, I fully expected Axel to accost me. It seemed to be the time of week he preferred to confront me, but he didn't. He ignored me as we left the class and went our separate ways. It was both a relief and a disappointment.

I chastised myself for feeling let down. I knew it was the bond wanting to be around him, but I couldn't control it. It's not like I wanted him to yell at me or say hurtful things to me, but the bond drew comfort from his proximity. I was glad it was only an extension of my soul. If it had its own desires and thoughts, it would be a nightmare. It clearly didn't understand that we'd been rejected by the thing it craved.

The rest of the week passed in the same manner. Axel ignored me but laughed in encouragement when one of his buddies said something rude about me.

Their comments were unoriginal.

Whore.

Skank.

Teacher fucker.

Stolen valor simp.

They were easy to ignore, and I let them roll off my back. The only ones that even remotely bothered me were those that involved my brother.

Mate-bond wrecker.

Night Heir ho.

Silver slut.

Puck fucker.

I cringed internally each time they taunted me about Puck, but I didn't let it show. Sidric, Jed, Brev, and Callie, on the other hand, weren't good at keeping quiet. They always snapped back, which only encouraged it, but I couldn't convince them to stop.

As the weeks passed, Callie and Jed grew busy with their new research project—me. I'd given them a couple of samples to experiment on, and after a particularly grueling day, I headed across campus to meet them. Autumn Equinox break would take me away from Araphel, and they both wanted to do some new tests.

I had my travel bag with me, planning to leave straight from Jed's lab.

"Hey!" Callie waved me in when she saw me through the door.

"Hi. You two look busy," I noted their appearance. They were in full lab garb, goggles and gloves included.

"Yeah, your little problem got our minds going, and we veered off to address other allergies using the same research. This is fucking great! We're going to blow minds when we're finished," Jed explained as he bustled around the room collecting and depositing whatever he was collecting and depositing.

"We're super excited," Callie beamed. "We need a couple of blood samples and several swabs from you today. Is that cool?"

"Absolutely." I dropped my bag and sat on a stool as they took what they needed from me. We chatted through the process, and they told me about their experiments and breakthroughs—none of which I understood enough to ever repeat.

"All set," Callie chirped, waving her hand over the little mark on my arm where she'd drawn my blood.

"When are you leaving?" I asked as I picked up my bag.

"Leaving for what?" Jed mumbled, not looking up from his task.

"Autumn Equinox break?"

They both snorted. "We're staying. That's why we wanted the samples. While everyone is gone, we'll have the whole lab to ourselves. We can work nonstop. We're not going anywhere," Callie informed me as she took my samples to the cooler.

"You're not taking a break? You two need to get some rest."

"Rest is for the wicked," Jed said, giving me a friendly wink.

"Well, don't forget to eat and sleep," I teased as I waved goodbye. Once outside, I set off for the secret portal that waited to take me home.

Chapter Fourteen

"There she is," Papa crooned as soon as I was through the portal. He was always the first one to greet or comfort me with anything.

"Hi, Papa." I let him pull me into his arms, hugging him tightly.

"How are you, my little princess?" The familiar scent of warm bark and pollen surrounded me as his breath tickled my head.

"Better now that I'm home."

"Stop hogging her," Pai demanded, rubbing my back. I released Papa and turned to hug him next. He was always a few degrees warmer than my other dads, and his dry, earthy scent reminded me of the court he hailed from—Summer. "We missed you," he whispered.

"I missed you all too. So much."

I was passed to Baba next, who grinned down at me. He pulled me into a quick embrace, and I inhaled the comforting aroma of dried leaves. "Hi, sweetheart," he said, kissing the top of my head.

He released me into Father's cool embrace, and even though my winter dad was physically colder and more serious than the others, his love was warm. "Welcome home, daughter."

My mother was last, and I held her the longest. She was soft and warm, and she smelled like all of her mates mixed with the comfort of night. "I want to know everything. Your brother said you've been having a hard time."

I sighed and nodded, willing myself not to cry. It didn't work. A few tears leaked out, and before I knew it, my dads had surrounded us in a family hug.

"I'm sorry," I sniffled against my mom's shoulder. I had been doing so well, but as they surrounded me with their comfort and love, my time away and the difficulty with Axel rushed to the surface.

"You have nothing to apologize for," Father said in a stern voice.

"I can't imagine what you're going through, sweetheart. I'm so sorry," my mother whispered in my ear before kissing my temple.

"We should have had that little shit expelled," Pai grumbled, and Papa hummed in agreement. Even Father added an approving grunt.

"As much as I agree, it would have drawn too much suspicion," Baba conceded.

He was right, and we all knew it.

"It's still a nice thought," Pai said.

"Lyra is holding her own," Puck said around a mouthful from the hallway. My mother released me, and I turned to look at my brother. We'd traveled through the portal together, but he'd slipped away to the kitchen for a snack when I greeted our parents.

He'd been able to come and go from home as he pleased, so his greeting was less enthusiastic than mine. I hadn't seen my parents in months, and even though we messaged, it wasn't the same.

"Lala's tougher than she looks," Puck said as he bit into the sandwich in his hand. "In fact, she's been handling herself better than me," he said around his mouthful of food.

Shea appeared behind him and smacked Puck on the back of the head. "Don't talk with your mouth full. We know all too well how badly you've been handling this situation. You're probably the one making it worse," Shea chided him and then pulled me into his side. "It was bad enough you switched the teams around, but the fighting needs to stop."

"Fuck that," Puck growled, wiping his mouth. "You don't know what it's like. You didn't hear what the asshole was saying."

"Enough," Father commanded, silencing the room. "Your desire to protect your sister is admirable, Puck, but Shea is right. You can't fight the Spring Noble."

Puck opened his mouth to argue, but Mother interrupted him. "They're right, son. As much as it pains me, you're taking it too personally."

"We should take it personally!"

"That's not what she means," Baba said with a smile. "Your mother simply means that you're taking it too personally for someone who isn't supposed to be directly involved. Acting out and letting it affect you all the time will draw attention. People will begin to wonder why you're so angry. What if the noble son starts to wonder why you're reacting after he says something to Lyra? He could question your motives."

"You're not supposed to know each other," Cleon added from the doorway where he stood. "The Spring Noble son knows what he did, and he knows Lyra is the female he did it to, but *you* aren't supposed to know that. He only knows you're mad that it happened."

Puck's shoulders slumped. "I know. It's been more difficult than I expected. I don't understand why he's being so cruel. Plus, I have to be around him all the time at practice and games."

"We sympathize," Father said, clapping him on the back. "Trust me. We wish we could've done something about it from the very beginning. If we could take away your sister's pain, we would in an instant. But you need to remember it isn't about you. It happened to her, and she needs you to support her, not make it worse. You have to rein it in."

Puck shook his head. "If you heard the things he says about her, you'd have a hard time too."

"It's probably best if we don't know the particulars," Baba growled, crossing his arms.

"Come on," Papa said, shouldering my bag. "Let's get Lyra settled. She doesn't need to deal with this at home."

Puck pulled me into a side hug as everyone dispersed. "Sorry, baby sister. I'll do better."

I patted his chest. "I know. We have to remember that what happened is what's best for the kingdom. In the end, that's all that matters." I gave him a watery smile. "If he'd accepted the bond and revealed his true nature afterward, our people would have suffered. My heart will mend, and our family will heal. That's what's important."

He rested his chin on my head. "You'll make an amazing queen one day, Lala. I'm proud to be your brother."

"We're all proud of you, daughter." I turned to find my parents and my brothers in the hallway, and their looks of adoration made me blush.

"Come on, sweet girl, get some rest before dinner." Papa held his hand out, and I released Puck to let my Summer Court dad escort me to my room.

The following morning, my family left me at home while they attended the Autumn Solstice gathering in town. As part of their duties, they had to make a public appearance, but we spent the rest of the day together when they returned. They caught me up on everything I'd missed, and I told them some more about my classes and the friends I'd made.

When it was time for dinner, the chef made sure all my favorite dishes were on the table. Luckily, we loved the same things, so no one felt put out. We laughed as we ate more than our fill, stuffing ourselves even further with dessert. After we changed into loungewear, we drank spiced rum around the fire.

It was wonderful.

Eventually, my parents excused themselves and my brothers dragged me into the game room, where they plied me with shots. We were all feeling a little tipsy when Shea pulled me to sit next to him on the couch, and the others left the game we were playing and joined us.

"All right, spill it, you two." He kicked his feet up, looking between Puck and me.

"I thought we were letting it go," Puck said with a sardonic smile. "You all said I was making it worse."

"Don't be a dick. You know damn well that everything we said earlier is valid. That doesn't mean I don't want to know."

I grumbled and pulled my legs up to my chest. "I don't think you want to know. Maybe we should just drop it."

Tunder sat forward, staring right at me. "Oh, now I really want to know, baby sister. We've only heard what Puck had to say. But obviously, there's more."

"What has Puck said?" I asked, turning to the brother in question. "What did you tell them?"

He shrugged. "Just what he said at the party. And what I've heard some of the guys say at practice."

"What guys? Who's saying what?"

He rolled his eyes. "Your Star Kicker had a few choice words for the Spring Noble. He said the douche accused him of stealing his spot on the team. Sidric thinks Axel talked shit about you to goad him into a fight. We all know that's not exactly true, but I let Sid believe it to be the case."

"And what he said to Puck at the party. Accusing you of being a mate breaker." Cleon added.

"That's not what he said," I grumbled.

"That's what he meant." Puck sneered. "If I hadn't been so offended at the insult, I would have puked."

"You're an idiot," Cleon said, shoving him.

Tunder lifted his brows. "So, tell us, Lala. What doesn't Puck know?"

I shook my head. "I don't want it to get worse, and it'll just piss you all off."

And it did. They fumed, talking over each other and making threats before I even said a thing.

"I'm going to tell mom she needs to have him pulled," Shea hissed.

"No, you're not." I turned to Shea. "You can't do that. None of you can do anything. He just calls me names, anyway. It's fine."

They all started shouting again.

"What names?"

"What did he call you?"

"How many times has this happened?"

"Why didn't you tell me?"

I groaned and dropped my head in my hands. "I love you all, but you're killing my buzz. I just want to forget about him for a couple of days."

They went quiet for a moment.

Cleon's voice was cautious when he asked, "Has he done anything ... else?"

I looked up at him. "Like what?"

"Threatened you?"

"Or been violent with you?" Tunder added.

I sighed and thought about how to answer. Apparently, that was the wrong thing to do. They took my pause as proof that Axel had done what they feared. "Stop! He hasn't done anything like that. Calm down. I would tell you if I was in danger. I'm not stupid."

They all shut up, shifting around uncomfortably.

"Look, he's cornered me a couple of times. He told me to leave the school, claiming it would be best if I weren't there. Obviously, that's not going to happen, and I told him as much. He hasn't threatened me, and he certainly hasn't hurt me physically. He's a jerk, but I think he's struggling with what's left of the bond. It's incredibly painful and uncomfortable to be around him, and if he's feeling the same way, then I understand why he's acting out." When they opened their mouths to argue, I held up my hands. "I'm not saying it's okay or that he has any right. I'm simply telling you I get why he doesn't want me around. It's making it harder for both of us."

They were quiet again as they thought about what I'd said, so I took my seat and picked up my drink, taking a long sip.

"What do you mean 'what's left of the bond'?" Shea asked.

My brows pulled together. "I don't know how to make it any clearer."

"You still feel the bond?" Tunder asked.

"What's left of it." I shrugged. "It's not strong, but it's not gone yet."

"That doesn't sound right." Shea tipped his head to the side as he looked at me.

"It's not like there are a lot of cases to compare it to," Cleon said as he sat back and crossed his ankle over his knee. "There are hardly any mate bond breaks in history. Perhaps it has to fade with time."

Shea and Tunder both hummed at his assessment.

"Maybe," Tunder sat back and took a long pull from his drink.

"At any rate, if he continues to harass you, you have to tell our parents—or administration," Puck said. "He can't be allowed to continue fucking with you. It's his fault, and he shouldn't get a pass."

"Hear, hear," Cleon said as they clinked their glasses.

Shea patted my leg. "You are handling it much better than I would have, but you can't suffer through his abuse just for the sake of it. If his bullshit doesn't stop, Lyra, you need to say something. You don't deserve his harassment."

"If he doesn't stop by the end of Starball season, you will say something," Tunder announced. "We're making a sibling pact on it."

I looked around at my brothers, who nodded in agreement.

"Fine." I held out my hand, and they all piled theirs on top. "If he doesn't stop bullying me by the end of Starball season, I will go to the administration and report him for harassment."

Binding magic tingled through my hand as we all agreed. If I didn't follow through willingly, the oath would force my hand—or in this case, my mouth.

With the deal made, we went back to drinking and chatting, and several hours later, we all stumbled to bed.

Chapter Fifteen

The rumor mill ran rampant after Autumn Equinox break. Evidently, Axel and Jana had gotten into a huge fight in the middle of the quad the day before I returned. The stories varied about what had happened, but everyone agreed that she'd tried to make him jealous. Whatever she'd done, it must have worked since they were hanging all over each other the following afternoon.

The recent development between them had an additional effect that I didn't understand: it added fuel to her ire for me. She became even more persistent in her name-calling. Every time I entered a room, she and her friends loudly proclaimed that I fucked teachers, citing my slutty ways as the reason I had such high marks.

At lunch, they called me *Starball team slut* and *mate breaker*. The latter was the one that got me. It annoyed me that they'd say something so disgusting and cruel. Not to mention, it was gross that they were saying it about my brother. But it downright pissed me off when Axel just sat there and let her accuse me of such a thing when he knew very well that if anyone was a mate breaker, it was him.

"Whatever, bitch." Callie flipped Jana off as we left lunch and headed to our Earth Grounding Rejuvenation class.

I wished it meant we were getting away from them for the day, but since Jana, Lacy, and Axel were all in the same class, it wasn't likely we would get any downtime that afternoon. The class was full, and I figured everyone needed to recover from the Autumn Equinox celebrations. Rejuvenation classes fell under self-study, and attendance was the only requirement as they were meant to help us connect with our magic. Mostly, they were a social block of time to relax and replenish.

Callie and I were making our way over the manicured lawn to the spot we favored when Jana and Lacy cackled, ramping up their attack on me once again.

"I doubt she'll mind since she spreads herself for half the team, anyway," Jana quipped.

I wasn't fast enough to counteract her elemental summons before vines lashed out at my body, ripping off my clothes. One of the ropey plants jerked my bag off my shoulder as two others grabbed my shirt, ripping it in half. Two more shredded my skirt until I was standing in front of the entire class in only my shoes, socks, and underwear.

The class went quiet as I looked down at myself in shock. Lacy and Jana howled with laughter at my near-naked state.

"What's the matter, slut?" Lacy snickered.

"What the fuck is wrong with you?" Callie whirled on them. "What is your problem?"

"Do you want to be next, bitch?" Jana hissed.

The vines moved toward Callie, but I struck before they had a chance.

I was pissed, and I didn't realize what the implications of my actions would be, but I hadn't had time to consider them before I acted. Flames roared to life, engulfing the vines and disintegrating them to ash before they could reach Callie. The snap of the flames was so fast and hot that Jana must have felt the backlash through her link with the earth, and she let out a high-pitched squeal.

The vines withered to dust, and a gust of wind blew them away, leaving nothing behind but burned grass. I wasn't sure if it was my wind that scattered the remains or if it was a coincidence, but it didn't matter. They were gone.

"What the fuck?" Jana yelled. "She attacked me! You all saw that she attacked me, right?"

It was quiet for a beat. Then, someone snorted. "That's not what I saw."

"Me either."

"You attacked her, Jana. She defended herself."

"If you play with fire, expect to get burned."

Jana stomped her foot and glared at the crowd. "You're going to defend the slut after she attacked me?"

"No one attacked you, dummy. Goddess, you're stupid."

I couldn't hide my smirk as I watched the scene unfold in front of me. Even though I was standing there half naked, I felt empowered by their defense of me. I was so happy they saw her for what she was—a bully and a brat.

"The whore is standing around in her underwear, and you're all blaming me!"

"That's called a bikini, you half-wit," Callie said as she whipped off her shirt. "All you did was save her time. We were going to get undressed to sunbathe, anyway."

It was true. Callie and I were both wearing bikinis under our uniforms, having fully intended to do what she'd said. I hadn't expected to be forcibly stripped in front of the entire class, however, and the fact I was still wearing my socks and shoes sort of made it obvious this hadn't been my intention. Even though it was a bikini, my socks and loafers made it feel inappropriate. But I owned it.

I shrugged and kicked off my shoes. "I liked that shirt, but thankfully, I have ten more just like it."

Callie chuckled next to me as she shimmied out of her skirt. We both peeled our socks off at the same time, shoving our clothes into our bags.

The students around us cheered and clapped, encouraging us as they made jokes about us stripping, but I knew it was all in good fun. They were making light of the situation, not being assholes like Jana and Lacy.

"Honey's got a nice ass," someone whooped.

Another yelled, "Go, little rabbit! Shake your tail!"

Callie shook her head but turned around and did just that, wiggling her ass for the crowd.

Jana crowed in frustration as her plan backfired spectacularly. She glowered at the other students, turning her glare on me before stomping away. I was pleased the students hadn't given her what she wanted. I was happy that everyone knew she was being a bully and instead of siding with her, they turned against her. As it should be.

She marched up to Axel, who stared at me with a heated expression. His gaze traveled up and down my body, finally landing on my face. I glared at him, and I could have sworn his lips twitched.

Jana yelled at him, but when he didn't immediately look at her, she shoved her hands against his chest. When he glanced down, whatever humor had been on his face dropped away, leaving a scowl behind.

She launched into a tirade, but I walked away, uninterested in hearing their fight. Callie and I went to our intended spot, where we sunbathed and laughed for the next couple of hours. Others came over and chatted with us, making jokes about what had happened, but I wasn't embarrassed. I welcomed the friendly conversation, feeling at ease for the first time all term.

Chapter Sixteen

I woke up feeling lighter than I had in a long time. A week had gone by since Jana destroyed my clothes at Earth Rejuvenation, and even though her antics hadn't stopped one bit, it didn't bother me. She was even crueler than before, and it was all because no one would join in her torment. She became a target for everyone's backlash, all while trying and failing to make my life unbearable.

They defended me and talked down to her. They shut her up when she called me names. When she tried to put me under for my ranking and top grades, they talked over her and congratulated me, asking for help with their assignments.

More and more people talked to me because of her constant abuse, and I found myself surrounded by friendly faces and conversation in class and during meals.

It felt amazing to have everyone defend me from the mean girl, even though I still didn't understand why she didn't like me. I almost felt grateful to the nasty female for what she had done since it was her actions that were responsible for my gregarious standing at Araphel Academy.

Callie and I sat down with our dinner plates as we waited for Sidric, Jed, and Brev. It was almost the end of another week, and the school was excited about the Starball team's winning streak. The Shadows were neck and neck with the Summer Court Hornets from High Crest Academy. There were only a handful of games left in the season before the Night Realm winning team would host the Day Realm winning team for the championship game. It also marked the end of the semester, and everyone was looking forward to the break after months of demanding coursework.

I was ahead in all my classes, and even though I enjoyed learning, I was eager for a reprieve. My brain was so full of new information that it felt heavy. Not to mention the stress of attending school with a rejected mate and his band of cheerleaders that put a strain on my everyday life.

The dining hall was packed. It was taco night, and based on how many people were there, it was a student favorite. They only served it once a month, and it was clear everyone wanted to partake. Even some instructors were in attendance, like Professor Warrock, who was chatting with Roko. They both gave me a nod when I smiled in their direction.

Callie and I grabbed tacos and a plate of nachos to share.

"They better hurry, or these are going to be gone," Callie said as she crunched on her bite happily.

I hummed in agreement. "They can get more," I told her after wiping a bit of cheese off my mouth.

"You missed a spot," Jana sneered.

We'd been so focused on our dinner that I hadn't noticed her arrival, which was impressive since she prided herself on making an entrance. Callie rolled her eyes, and we turned to look at her.

"What do you want?" Callie snapped, letting Jana know exactly how she felt about her.

I preferred to ignore her, and I rarely rose to the bait. After I'd destroyed her vines in Earth Rejuvenation, I'd been indifferent. Someday, when my identity was no longer a secret, I wouldn't want to face backlash from our encounters. There were plenty of witnesses that could attest that I'd never been the aggressor, but it wasn't becoming of me to argue or fight with another student. I would stand up for myself, but there was no reason for me to make it worse.

"Everyone else might buy the sweet act, but I know what you really are," Jana hissed. She gave me a sarcastic smile and threw the contents of her cup on my shirt, drenching me with water. "A sticky slut." She over-enunciated the word, staring pointedly at my now see-through top, and flipped her hair over her shoulder as she sauntered away.

I stood and wiped at my shirt, but there was nothing I could do—I was drenched, and I couldn't use my wind magic to dry myself. Everyone knew I only had earth, and after accidentally burning Jana's vines, they assumed I was earning an affinity for fire. But I couldn't give anything else away. Not even for a wet shirt that was showing off my lacy bra to half of the student body and faculty.

I was shocked and angry, knowing her actions were because of Axel. I simply couldn't understand why he wouldn't leave me alone. Why did he keep instigating all of this? His hatred was the root cause of everything. He'd lost his position on the Starball team because of it, and instead of taking responsibility and accepting the consequences, he targeted Sidric as a way to target me. Why that gave Jana permission to exact his revenge on me, I didn't know. It made little sense, but here I was at the end of another encounter while they all laughed at my misfortune.

Turning, I found him and his table of friends making a scene at my expense. They had huge smiles on their faces as they high-fived and fist-bumped each other, whistling and waggling their eyebrows up and down at my exposed skin. Axel made a big show of looking at my breasts—or rather, my white lace bra—through the wet fabric.

"That fucking asshole." Callie stood and threw her napkin down on her plate. "What is your problem?" she yelled across the dining hall, but all that did was draw more attention to me and my wet top. Not everyone had seen what happened, but now the whole room knew. The dining hall fell quiet as the other students took in the scene.

I grabbed a napkin and looked down at myself, intending to soak up what I could, but I paused when I smelled something sweet. Lifting my arm, I took a deep inhale.

"What's the matter, *honey*?" Jana taunted.

I watched her tip her head back in an exaggerated laugh. I looked at Axel, not sure what to expect, but I found him enjoying himself at my expense. Jana's comment didn't make sense to me at first—until it did.

I wasn't angry anymore.

I was scared.

I felt the blood drain from my face. Whatever he saw in my features made him sit up higher and shuttered his smile.

I turned to Callie. She'd figured it out just as I did, and panic washed over her face.

"No." She scrambled away from her side of the table and rushed over, yanking at my shirt. "Get it off," she yelled.

But it was too late. My throat was thick. My next breath was a wheeze, and my skin was overly warm.

"Get it off, Lyra," Callie yelled again, and whatever chatter and laughter still filled the room dropped into silence.

I clawed at the buttons as she ripped away the fabric. My skin was on fire, and my throat was swelling, but we pulled the shirt off my body.

"Water. I need water," Callie yelled again and grabbed our glasses and dumped them on me. I shook my head as she used the liquid and napkins to scrub the honey from my skin.

"What's going on?" Professor Warrock asked from across the room.

"I... can't..." I gasped, frantically clawing at my throat. "Cal..."

"Shit, shit, shit." Callie pushed her hand against my chest and forced me to sit down, yelling over her shoulder, "Get a healer! I need a healer!"

I looked into her frantic eyes as the room exploded around me. Shouts filled the space, and chairs and table legs squeaked across the floor. Shadowy figures surrounded me.

"What's wrong with her?" Axel yelled.

I didn't know why he cared—it was his fault. However, his voice came through to me loud and clear.

I knew I must have looked like a fish out of water as I gasped for breath, but I couldn't help it. My skin was on fire, and my vision blurred at the edges.

"What happened to her?" Sidric's voice boomed next to me as he wrapped his hands around my face. "Lyra, honey, breathe."

I scratched at my throat and chest. I couldn't get air, and I shook my head as tears filled my eyes and my chest caved as I struggled for air. My body trembled as shock took over. Callie forced her healing magic into me, and Roko appeared beside her, placing his hands alongside hers.

"What is wrong with her?" Axel roared as Sidric yelled at me to breathe. "Tell me what's wrong!"

"She's allergic to honey, you fucking asshole," Callie screamed, bursting into tears. "I'm not strong enough," she whimpered.

"I'll do what I can, but I'm not a healer," Roko said, furrowing his brow.

My eyes rolled, and Sidric pressed his lips to mine as my head lolled to the side. He whispered, "Lyra, come on, baby, you gotta breathe."

My consciousness dimmed, and I was only slightly aware of the chaos around me.

"It's not working."

"Where's the healer?"

"What's happening to her... Is she..."

"Holy shit..."

"Get back! Everyone step back now!"

"Lyra... Oh goddess..."

"She's dying..."

"No! Let me through!"

"She can't be..."

"My gods..."

"Keep them away."

"... move her ..."

"We must!"

"I'm taking..."

I couldn't keep track of who was speaking as I faded in and out. Someone lifted me into their arms, and air whipped past my body. The uproar quieted until only a few hushed voices remained. A bright light filtered through my eyelids as I was jostled from side to side. More voices. More commands. More pleading.

Still no breath.

Then, darkness.

Chapter Seventeen

It was dark when I felt a calloused hand slip into mine. Their skin was warm, or perhaps mine was ice-cold, but it felt nice either way. They squeezed my hand tight, and something soft pressed against my fingers, once, twice, three times. My hand moved again, then pressed against something warm and hard like a forehead. I couldn't be sure. I was mostly asleep and could be dreaming all of it. I faded, even as I struggled to place the voice whispering, "Please. Please don't die. Please be okay, my Lyra." More kisses were brushed over my skin. "I can't do this... I'm so sorry. I didn't want this. I didn't want to do this. Please get better. Please... I can't lose..."

A loud bang interrupted the quiet peace, and darkness pulled me under.

When I awoke, I was so warm and comfortable that I knew I was at home in my bed. I rolled over and stretched as I tried to remember what had happened. As my memories trickled in, I sat up with a start, pressing a hand to my neck.

My skin had been on fire and my throat swollen shut.

I'd thought I was going to die.

I remembered gasping for air and shaking as darkness had taken over. Callie had tried to help, and Roko too. Maybe even Sidric?

But how had I gotten home?

I climbed out of bed and stumbled to the bathroom to change. I felt a little wobbly on my feet, so I'd likely been in bed for a couple of days. I pulled on loungewear since I was home—as well as recovering from an anaphylactic episode—and after brushing my teeth and combing through my hair, I left in search of my family.

I wasn't sure what time it was, but based on the smells coming from the dining room, I guessed it was breakfast. The smell of coffee and pancakes lured me down the hall, and I perked up when I heard voices. The scraping of silverware against plates was a giveaway they were still eating.

I couldn't hear what they were saying, but the conversation was quiet and subdued. A laugh cut through the hushed room, making me smile. I must not have been too terribly close to death for them to feel so at ease.

Rounding the corner, I opened my mouth to tease them when I screeched and turned around, covering my face before attempting to scurry back out through the threshold. I didn't make it.

"Lyra," Puck called. Chairs scraped against the floor, drowning out his voice.

Tunder spun me around and crushed me in his embrace. "Don't you ever do that to us again," he growled, his deep voice demanding and desperate.

Puck hugged me from behind, squishing me between the two of them. "I'm so glad you're awake."

"Don't hog her," Cleon complained as he circled his arms around the three of us.

"You guys are making this more difficult than it needs to be," Shea chided, but he followed suit, wrapping his arms around the group. "You scared us, baby sister."

They bombarded me with questions before I could ask them what the hell was going on.

"How are you feeling? Are you dizzy?"

"Should you be up? I don't think you should be up yet."

"Are you hungry? I bet you're hungry."

"She needs to drink something. You're thirsty, right?"

"You should go back to bed; we'll bring you breakfast there."

"Can you walk? I can carry you."

"Can you breathe okay? Shit, we shouldn't be hugging you!"

"We can hug her. She can breathe, right? You can breathe?"

"All right, that's enough," Father said as I heard snickering in the background. "You four are smothering her."

"She almost died," Puck argued, but the four of them stepped back. Not by much, just enough to give me a little breathing room.

"Well, she didn't, and that doesn't mean you can squish her." Pai clicked his tongue. "Now, move."

He pushed his way between my brothers and pulled me into a bone-crushing hug of his own.

"You just said not to squish her," Puck argued.

"Calm down, son," Baba said, tutting as his warm hand rubbed my back.

"Yes, please. You've been an absolute nightmare for three days. You can calm down now," Papa said.

More snickering came from the table, and I peeked up at Father. "I shouldn't be here. What's happening?" I whispered.

He smiled at me and gave my chin a little pinch. "We have a lot to talk about."

"My beautiful girl." Mother snaked her arms around me, and I held her tight. "Please don't scare me like that again, sweet girl."

"I didn't mean to."

"I know, darling." She kissed my head as her voice cracked. "I know it wasn't your fault. You were very lucky."

"You've clearly made some amazing friends," Father said.

"Are you hungry?" Mother pulled back to look at me. Her eyes were swimming with tears, but she had a smile on her face.

"Thirsty mostly, but yes. I'm hungry too."

"Okay." She nodded and turned me to face the room.

"Mother," I screeched, hiding my face again.

"It's all right, dear. They know."

"What?" I whispered, peeking at her through my fingers.

The rest of my family had returned to their seats, so it was just me and mom standing at the head of the table—facing all of my friends.

Callie, Sidric, Jed, Brev, Roko, and Professor Warrock were scattered around our family dining table and watching us with rapt interest.

Mother walked me over to an empty seat. She kissed the top of my head and whispered that everything was fine. In a louder voice, she explained, "As your life essence faded, the magic that held your glamour withered away. Your friends, your brother's mate, and professor Warrock were all surrounding you when it happened. There was nothing they could do to stop it, so they protected you by keeping everyone away and moving you to a healer. Their quick thinking and unquestionable loyalty have preserved your identity. They are the only ones that know who you truly are, and they have been sworn to secrecy under the same geas as the rest of us." She smiled at the group as they stared at me like I'd grown another head.

Then, they all stood as one and dropped their heads in supplication.

"Oh goddess, don't do that," I complained, earning snorts from my brothers and fathers.

"You're the freaking Night Princess. We have to! It's like, the rules," Callie whispered with a flustered voice.

"Please stop." I stepped up to her and grasped her arms.

She looked up at me with wide, beautiful, warm eyes filled with tears. "Oh, Lyra, I thought you were going to..." Her breath caught as her lip quivered.

I pulled her into a tight hug. "You saved me. Thank you." She shook her head, but I wouldn't hear it. "No, Callie, you did. Whatever you did in those first few minutes saved me."

"It wasn't just me," she sniffled. "Roko helped bolster my healing. The others kept everyone away, and Mr. Warrock ran you to the master healers' room."

I pulled away, heading to Roko next. "Thank you." I hugged him tightly.

"I did what I could. Callie really deserves your thanks. She's being modest."

"I know." I giggled. "Still, thank you." I pulled back with a smile. "I'm so glad I can know you now for real. You're the first of my brother's mates I've had the privilege of meeting. Now, you're officially my brother too."

His eyes swam. "By the goddess, I knew I loved you. I just didn't understand why. It makes so much sense now. All of it. Especially why this one was so angry all the time." He elbowed Puck playfully and hugged me again. "I always knew I'd meet you one day, but I'm so happy it's you."

"Well, this doesn't seem right. I want our mates to meet her now," Cleon grumbled impishly. "And my mate is a master healer. I feel robbed."

"And tell me, brother, what perils would you put our dear sister in to make that happen?" Shea teased.

"Maybe let's not joke about your sister's life, hmm?" Father didn't sound amused.

My brothers bickered amongst themselves, so I turned to the others. I thanked Jed and Brev, giving each of them a hug before moving to Professor Warrock.

"Professor." I reached out my hand. "Thank you for saving my life."

He winked. "Princess, it was my honor. I'd rather not do it again, but now that I'm in the know, you can rest assured that my watchful eye will be even keener than before."

I shook my head, giggling. He was an incorrigible flirt, but I didn't mind. If I hadn't met Sidric, I'm quite certain I would have taken a more intimate interest in my professor.

I turned to Sidric, who was watching me intensely.

"Sidric." I stepped into his personal space.

"Princess." He gave me a crooked smile. "Or may I still call you honey?" He arched a brow, lifting his finger to tap on his lip. "Hmm, perhaps princess honey?"

"Shh, my parents will hear you." I blushed.

"I didn't know it was possible," he said as he ran a finger under my chin. "But you're even more beautiful than you were before."

"Thank you for saving my life, Sidric." I wrapped my arms around him and thanked him before he could embarrass me even further. It was bad enough that Puck knew of my relationship—I didn't want the others to know too.

Sidric held me close and breathed in the scent of my hair. "I know you're not my mate. I've always been disappointed by that, but watching you ... suffer... Lyra, I'm so glad you're okay. I'm quite fond of you."

"I'm fond of you too. Thank you for being there."

His eyes flicked to my lips, and he glanced at my family at the other end of the table. He leaned down and whispered in my ear, "I'll show you how thankful I am when I get you alone." He released me, pressing a kiss to my cheek.

"No need to pretend, we are well aware of your relationship." Pai smirked and winked at me. "She's had my blessings to sow her wild oats since she left for the academy. I'm happy she took my advice."

"Dad!" I dropped my head in my hands as the others laughed.

"Not at family dinner, dear," Mother chided. "Lyra, my love, please sit and eat. You've been resting for several days, and you need to get your strength back."

It wasn't a command, but every one of my friends jumped into action at her decree.

Sidric pulled out a chair and directed me to sit down. Jed grabbed a glass, Brev filled it with water, and Callie dished eggs and pancakes onto my plate. Roko put a napkin on my lap, and Professor Warrock chuckled as he watched with humor in his gaze.

"If you thought there were rumors regarding your relationships before, princess, you might want to prepare yourself. Nearly dying and revealing yourself to your friends will not curb gossip."

Chapter Eighteen

"I want you to go back to bed and rest, daughter." Father was the last to hug me as my parents said goodbye to my friends and excused themselves for the evening. "You're still recovering, and you need sleep before we'll even consider allowing you to return to school."

"Yes, Father." I hugged him, and he kissed the top of my head before releasing me into my mom's embrace.

"Goodnight, my sweet girl. Don't push yourself or stay up too late. Listen to your father."

"I will."

"Good." She smiled at me and turned to the room. "Good night, everyone. We expect to see you all again for breakfast before you go."

The group murmured their assent.

"I'm also heading to bed." Professor Warrock inclined his head and followed my parents out of the room.

All at once, everyone turned to face me. "What?"

"Let's go to the game room." Puck grabbed my hand and pulled me down the hall.

When we arrived, everyone grabbed drinks, but I was only allowed a glass of water. "You guys are lame," I complained.

"You almost died. Drink your water and be grateful." Tunder sat next to me.

"So, you all have been staying here?"

"Yes," they chorused.

"Your family has been very welcoming," Jed said, smiling at my brothers as he put his arm around Callie.

"You helped my sister. We can never repay you for what you did." Shea shifted around in his chair and crossed an ankle over his knee.

My brothers all agreed, each saying their own version of his statement.

"How is this going to work?" Brev asked. "Now that we all know. We're under the geas, and even if we wanted to divulge your secret—which we do not—we couldn't. I understand that, but the dynamic will surely change, won't it?"

"No." Puck shook his head. "You'll all need to keep up appearances and act as you've always done in the past. Any deviation in your behavior will cause suspicion. By that, I mean you can't bow or go out of your way as protocol would normally require."

"I would like to be friends with your sister. Is that allowed? We were already moving toward that before all this happened," Roko said, wrinkling his brow.

"I'd like that. She's your sister now, too, remember?" Puck beamed at his mate. "I just mean that you can't let the knowledge of who she truly is affect your interactions."

Cleon snorted. "Because you've done so well with that yourself, brother?"

"That's different."

"Not really, but please go on."

"Asshole," Puck grumbled, and my friends looked around the room in confusion.

"What are we missing?" Sidric asked from my other side. "We should know everything that involves Lyra at school. Otherwise, we could make a mistake."

"Not likely." Shea shook his head. "Whether or not you realized it while being spelled with the geas, you cannot disclose any information about my sister that wasn't part of her hidden identity."

"I knew it. I told you." Brev scooted forward and smacked Jed's knee. "We agreed to not discuss any mating revelries in the past, present, or future." Brev looked at Puck. "That's what Cleon meant. The rumors about Axel and Spring Equinox are true. He really rejected his mate, and that's why you don't like him. Ha!" He clapped once.

He wasn't wrong, but he hadn't pieced it all together. My brothers and I stiffened, and the room stayed quiet for a beat too long before Callie sucked in a breath.

"Oh my goddess, Lyra." She sat up and rushed over to me with tears in her eyes. "That's not true, is it? Please tell me it's not true. That's why he's been so awful to you?" I smiled as her lips quivered. "No..." She pulled me into the gentlest hug I'd ever received, holding me as if any pressure at all would break me to pieces.

Sidric went rigid next to me. "Are you fucking kidding me? That son of a bitch!"

"Shit. Lyra," Brev rambled. "Fuck. I didn't... You can't be... Shit. I didn't mean... I didn't know... Ow! Fuck, I didn't know!"

"You stupid shit, why do you always have to open your mouth?" Jed ground out, punching Brev in the arm.

"Fuck, I didn't know! How was I supposed to know? Puck said that he was pissed because it *could* have been his sister! Not that it was!"

They started arguing, and Roko must have been upset, too, because Puck comforted him quietly.

"It's all right," I said, releasing Callie.

"The fuck it is," Sidric roared. "How dare he! Who in their right mind rejects their fated mate?"

"The Spring Court asshole, evidently," Professor Warrock said from the doorway, and we all turned to look at him. "My apologies, I didn't mean to eavesdrop nor overhear. I only came for a nightcap. However, I'm glad I did. I think it's relevant for us to know. Adding the mating revelries to the geas made sense to me and I didn't question it, but now I understand why."

"It changes nothing," Tunder said. "The rumors surrounding the Spring Equinox are true, but it's a moot point. People didn't need to know it was Lyra he rejected, and now that you've pieced it together, it doesn't change anything. Nor does it impact how you behave going forward."

"Of course not." Professor Warrock nodded and poured himself a drink. "It clears up my confusion, though. I didn't understand his attitude toward Lyra. It didn't seem likely that it was all because of Sidric."

"Do you think Jana knows? Is that why she's targeting you?" Callie asked as she wiped her eyes.

"Jana's just a bitch." Jed shook his head. "If not for Lyra, she would have targeted someone else."

"Only if Axel looked twice at them," Brev added. "For someone who chose something so atrocious, he can't seem to let it go. All the attention he gave you made her jealous."

"He doesn't give me attention." I shook my head.

"Not that you've noticed," Sidric huffed. "But he has. He's always watching you. Now, I understand why.

"Negative attention is still attention," Callie agreed.

"Yes, but it's more than that. As far up his ass as she is, Jana would have noticed a change in Axel. She's been acting out of jealousy."

"He wouldn't have told her, though," Puck said. "Not unless he wanted everyone to know the rumors were true. Even Jana wouldn't stick by his side if people found out. He'd be a social pariah."

"I agree," Professor Warrock said. "Rejecting your fated mate is nearly unheard of. He's struggling to deal with the rumors, so he'd never give her that kind of ammunition. Not for fear of her blabbing, but for the leverage she'd have over him. She's her father's daughter through and through, and she'd use any advantage to her favor."

"I can't believe you put that asshole on my team," Roko complained. "I know you couldn't tell me why, and I would have done it for you anyway, but dammit, Puck!"

"I'm sorry. I know it wasn't fair, but having him on my team, speaking to me every day..." He growled. Actually growled. "I couldn't do it."

"I know." Roko hugged him. "I understand, but I'm still mad about it."

"If it helps, it's a good thing he's not on Silver. I don't know if I could resist kicking his ass at practice every single fucking day myself," Sidric said in a low voice. "Maybe you shouldn't have told us. All I can think about now is smashing that prick's face in."

I put my hand on his knee. "That won't help anything. Listen, you guys are taking this too hard. It's been over half a year now."

"How are you even going to school with him?" Callie asked, squeezing my hand. "I don't know how you're doing this, Lyra."

My brothers shifted in their seats.

Shea cleared his throat. "I don't know how she's doing it, either. She's stronger than I am."

The others grunted in agreement.

"I couldn't do it." Roko's voice broke as he looked at my brother. "Is it awful that I hate him?"

Puck snorted. "Fuck no. It's the least that asshole deserves."

Tunder cut in, saying, "Let's get back to the original topic. You all need to deal with this new reality of yours because you have to act as if nothing has changed when you go back." He looked around the room, meeting everyone's gaze. "Your future queen's anonymity depends on it. It is not an effortless task for Lyra, us, or her future bond mates—the ones that will prove worthy—but it must be done. The balance of power and the strength of their bonds is the very foundation of our realms, and it is our duty to ensure that for her and us all."

Chapter Nineteen

My friends returned to campus after breakfast the following morning, but I planned to spend an additional night at home. It was near the end of the week when Jana had thrown honey water on me, so I'd only missed one day of classes.

The story was that I'd been taken home after going to a healing facility. The others would claim that they'd gone home for the weekend as well. If prodded further, they would say that the administration advised them to get away for the weekend to deal with the stress and trauma of watching their friend nearly die.

It was a good story and not entirely a lie.

I was hesitant to go back, but not because I feared the whispers or questions about what had happened. I was just reluctant to return. My healer explained that it was perfectly normal. I had been through a traumatic event; I'd nearly died, and I was going back to the place it happened. It was natural to feel this way.

I knew I couldn't hide away forever, and I didn't want to. There were things I needed to do, and cowering behind castle walls wouldn't accomplish them. So, I pulled up my bootstraps—metaphorically speaking—and went back to school.

After I arrived via portal, Puck and Roko met me just outside the secret alcove. Callie was there, too, which I wasn't expecting, but I was incredibly grateful to see her.

"We realized it might look a little suspicious if just the two of us were seen escorting you back to your dorm," Roko whispered as we hugged. "Callie came along to help."

"As if you could keep me away." She shoved him playfully and took his spot, wrapping me up in her arms.

We walked through the quad, and a few people stopped us to express their concerns about what had happened. Each of them seemed grateful I was okay. While I was gone, a notice had gone out to all staff and students, reminding them of the zero-tolerance bullying policy. It was a little embarrassing, but I agreed with the reminder. No one should be scared to attend school. It was ridiculous that it needed to be said at all, considering we were all adults. This wasn't grade school, for crying out loud. After we left the academy, we would enter the work field and become contributing—and hopefully, productive—members of society.

"I never asked, but what happened to Jana?"

"Not nearly enough," Puck grumbled.

"She was transferred to her home court school," Roko told me.

"The parentals wanted her expelled, but her family—or more specifically, her father—is a high-ranking noble in the Spring Court. He used his position and convinced the Queen that his daughter should be granted a second chance. He petitioned to have her sent to Valley Hill Academy instead of ending her advanced education," Puck told me quietly. "If she could have divulged who the target was that his precious daughter attacked, the conversation would have gone differently, I'm sure."

I gave him a tight smile. "At least she's not here."

"I heard she was upset when she found out about your allergy. Not that it's an excuse or anything, but she wasn't trying to kill you. She made sure everyone knew that," Callie said. "She wanted to apologize, but she was only given enough time to pack her things and leave. She was heard blubbering and blustering to anyone who would listen while being escorted off the property."

"I wouldn't have wanted to see her. I don't think I'm ready to accept an apology—even if it's true," I added, disbelief weighing heavily on my tone.

"You don't have to worry about her or her friends." Roko opened the door to my building. "Jana was the instigator. They were keeping to themselves this morning at practice."

Meira and Lacy were on the cheerleading squad together, and they practiced at the same time as the Starball players.

"I wouldn't be surprised if they transferred or tried to redeem themselves in the eyes of the other students and try to find a new friend group. Jana wasn't very nice to them, either," Puck added as the elevator doors closed. "But they deserve whatever comes their way for going along with it and joining in."

"They won't get any sympathy from me." Callie huffed.

When we reached my room, they all hugged me before they left. I was glad I had some time alone to readjust to being back. I knew I'd been only gone for a short time, but it seemed longer. I felt raw and exposed all over again, so I hoped having time to acclimate would help.

I slept better than I'd expected, waking up less nervous than I'd been the night before. I was supposed to meet Callie and the others for breakfast, but she had barely rolled out of bed and I desperately needed coffee, so I told her she could meet me downstairs when she was ready.

Several students bustled through the halls, so I didn't feel like a total swotter being up and ready for class so early. I was out the door of my building, across campus, and moving down the long corridor to the dining hall when Axel came up next to me.

"Lyra?" He spoke my name quietly, but it didn't matter. I jerked away from him and sucked in a breath as I spun to face him. "I didn't mean to scare you," he said, raising his hands.

I flinched and shuffled backward until my body hit the wall, pulling my hands up to my chest protectively.

His eyes were so wide I could see white all around his irises. He looked horrified. "Lyra..." His voice was so quiet and laced with some emotion I couldn't place. "I'm not going to hurt you."

He made a move like he was going to come closer, and I flinched again, turning my face as if to hide from him. It was stupid. I had magic, and I knew I could defend myself, but my fear of being attacked made me shut down. After Jana's assault, I knew what it felt like to be helpless.

"Oh goddess." His voice was barely a whisper. "Lyra, oh... Lyra, my... I would never hurt you. I'm so sorry..."

I opened my eyes and looked at him, frozen with panic. He looked distraught as he backed away and sat on the ground. His legs were bent, and his elbows rested on his knees as he dropped his head into his hands. He pushed his fingers through his hair and stared up at me.

"I'm so sorry. I didn't know. I didn't know she was going to do that. I didn't know you were allergic... I..."

"What do you want?" My voice wasn't strong, but I got the words out without breaking.

"I'm so sorry. Please... Please forgive me."

I shook my head. "Your girlfriend nearly killed me." That time, my voice broke. "Because of you." My eyes swam, and my vision blurred as tears fell down my face. I didn't want to cry, but that was the truth of it. She'd targeted me because of him.

"I'm so, so sorry..." He shook his head as his eyes bounced around my face, watching the tears slide down my cheeks. "I never wanted this to happen... Lyra, please... Oh goddess. What have I done? What have I done to you... I'm so sorry..."

He kept repeating himself, and I didn't want to hear it anymore.

"You need to leave me alone, Axel," I begged. "I almost died because of you. Why are you doing this to me? You chose this... Please leave me alone." My breath caught.

His eyes filled with tears, and they leaked down his face as his breathing hitched. I didn't understand. Logically, I knew he hadn't tried to kill me. I didn't think I was actually afraid of him, but I was still raw and healing from the trauma of the attack. And regardless, he was the root cause. It was his fault, even if he wasn't the one to throw the drink.

"I'm so sorry, my ... Lyra," he whispered again.

The agony on his face and the way he rubbed his chest told me we were both feeling the painful frays of our broken bond. My heart always ached around him, but seeing him suffer was excruciating.

It should have been enough to sever the bond, but it wasn't. The ache followed me around long after I fled, and I didn't see him for the rest of the day or even the rest of the week.

Chapter Twenty

The Araphel Academy Shadows won the night division once again, so our school was hosting the Starball Dusk to Dawn Championship. As the defending champions, we were awarded the home-field advantage. The campus was packed with students, staff, and alumni from all over the Night Realm, making it a bustling hub of activity. The Starball teams from each seasonal court and realm were attending in support. Araphel housed all the students while everyone else stayed in town.

All in all, it was very exciting.

There were tons of parties all over on and off campus. Class was dismissed early for the long weekend as most students intended to skip anyway, and the staff seemed just as eager to participate.

It had only been a couple of weeks since the honey incident, but I'd moved past the shock of it all. It helped that Jana wasn't around, and even though she'd sent me flowers and an apology, I was still grateful she wasn't here. Her friends had dropped off the map too. They were still at Araphel, but they were scarcely seen.

Axel was the same.

If I saw him at all, it was very brief. In our shared classes, he moved to the back and stayed out of my line of sight. He came in late and was always the first to leave. If I ever saw him at meals, he quickly disappeared, even if he hadn't finished eating. If we happened to be in the same area, he'd give me a wide berth or disappear around the next corner, or down a different hall.

I appreciated that he was giving me the space that I'd asked for—the space that he'd wanted, originally.

I knew my response to him that first day had been because I was still recovering from what happened, and while it'd been an overreaction, I wasn't embarrassed. I still believed it was because of him I'd been targeted by Jana and her friends, but I wasn't holding a grudge. I didn't necessarily forgive him, but I wasn't spiteful about it.

The bond between us was still there in shreds, and while it hurt to avoid him, it also helped in its own way. I was almost certain that if we kept our distance, the link between us would finally break.

My friends had all settled into the knowledge of my identity. At first, they'd been stiffer and more formal than before, but each time I pointed it out and reminded them it wasn't necessary, they stopped. Eventually, they'd eased and fallen back into our natural state.

I was glad that Roko had been in the dining hall when the incident happened. Because he'd been the one to help me, the other students accepted our new friendship. Now that I was friends with my brother's mate, I could spend time with Puck without it drawing attention. All in all, there were positive side effects of the traumatic event.

There was a huge party the night before the big game for the team. All the other court teams were invited, plus students from each academy. It was the premier event of the season. I'd heard about them from my brothers for years, and I was so excited to finally go to one.

I wore my vintage Starball shirt again, but I'd opted out of face paint when Callie had suggested it. I'd let her put some sparkles under my eyes, though.

"First, we'll grab a drink, before we find Jed, Sidric, and Brev," she informed me as we left our building. "Once we find them, we'll be glued to their sides all night, and I want to explore!"

There would be food, drinks, games, and a DJ. It was not our average Starball kegger—it was a legit party with all the trimmings.

"We have to eat," I told her. "Last time we went out, we were both drunk off two beers. So, the first stop is food, then we get a drink."

She rolled her eyes. "Fine. But yeah, you're right." She giggled. "Though, I had no complaints after the party."

"Same." I gave her a side eye, and we burst into laughter.

The party was on the far side of campus, close to the lake where Callie and I had spent one of our first outings together. The music was already pumping, and you could feel the bass through the ground as you walked. It was loud, but not loud enough that you couldn't have a conversation. Tents were offering every type of food you could think of, and drink stations and fire pits were scattered around the clearing.

We went to the food tables first, just like we'd planned. We both grabbed sliders and a plate of smothered curly fries to share. It was a greasy, messy, delicious mess. When we finished, we went to the first keg we could find and filled up two glasses of cold frothy beer each. One was to quench our thirst and wash down the food we'd stuffed ourselves with, and the other was to enjoy while we meandered through the crowd.

There were tables with beads, hair pom-poms, stickers, hats, t-shirts, and bags. I grabbed a beer cozy to keep my hands from freezing. Callie did the same, but she also loaded up on everything else. She was a walking Starball advertisement by the time she was finished. I let her put some beads around my neck when she pouted at my lack of school spirit.

Even though all the students wore their home team colors, shirts, and jerseys, there was nothing but camaraderie among the crowd. There weren't imaginary borders between us, but there were still larger gatherings of students who stuck with their own classmates. That was to be expected, though, and it made it easier for us to locate our friends and team.

I saw dozens of people wearing our colors, and I knew we were getting close. I even felt a draw toward the crowd. There was a lot of cheering and general excitement coming from our peers.

"What are they doing?" Callie asked as we stood on our tiptoes to try and get a better look.

"Introducing the players like they do at games. It's a bit more dramatic since they all show off," someone next to us answered, cheering loudly when they called out another name.

"Let's get closer." I grabbed Callie's hand, and we weaved through the crowd.

Puck was announcing everyone on his team, and when he saw us break through the large circle, he waved. When he announced Brev, Callie and I hooted for him with the others. Then he called Jed, and Callie jumped up and down as she screamed for him. She sloshed her beer, and I laughed at her antics. Sidric was next, and I followed suit, though I kept my drink inside my cup. He winked at me after doing a backflip.

The Black team gathered and formed a circle, chanting and jumping up and down in some sort of bro-dance. It was awesome. Afterward, they stood off to the side as Puck announced Roko, and I cheered like crazy with the crowd. He announced his team, and by the end, my throat was sore.

When it came time for him to announce Axel, I felt a spike of something in my chest, but I ignored it. I refused to dwell on or think about it during the festivities. I didn't go all out and holler for him, but I clapped with the others. My smile felt forced, so I pulled Callie into a chat instead of watching him as he grandstanded for the crowd.

Callie scowled in his direction, but she smiled at me, knowing I needed her attention and support.

"We'll get more beers when they're done," I told her. "Since you spilled yours all over the place."

"Some for me, some for the homies." She sipped what little was left in her cup before dumping the drops out onto the ground.

Puck took over again when the Black Squad finished their own chants and round romp. Then they all banged on their chest afterward, which was kind of hilarious. I couldn't help but laugh at the ridiculousness of it all.

I accidentally caught Axel's eye, feeling another jolt when he smiled at me. He looked away quickly and put himself behind the others, out of my sight once more.

We waved to the guys and prepared to find more drinks when someone rolled a keg into the open space, saving us the effort.

"Sweet!" Callie jumped up, grabbing my hand and pulling me toward the front of the line. "Two, please." She smiled sweetly at the massive dude pouring drinks.

"Two for the pretty lady, coming right up," he grinned at her. He wore a Stallions jersey from Ebymm Academy—the Autumn Court school.

"We were almost celebrating you guys," Callie beamed at him.

"Next year, baby." He handed her the drinks. "Now that the Night Duke is graduating, we'll have a shot."

"I wouldn't be so sure." Puck clapped him on the back and held out his empty cup for a refill. "My replacement will be better than me by next season."

"Ha!" The guy smiled. "You haven't seen our new captain yet. We're taking the championship next year. You'll see."

"Oh yeah, and where is this new captain?" Roko looked around as if said person would jump out and introduce himself.

"Ah, he couldn't get away. But you'll see him soon enough, Roko." He clapped my brother's mate on the back in a friendly gesture.

"You Stoppers are all the same. Big muscles and big talk." Puck puffed up his chest as he teased the huge male.

He wasn't wrong. The Offensive and Defensive Stoppers were some of the largest players on the team. Their physical strength wasn't the only thing they used on the field, but it sure helped.

He laughed, and it was such a pure sound I couldn't help but look up at him and smile. My chest pulsed again like the bond was trying to break free. I gasped, attempting to catch my breath, but I heard Axel's voice raise over the crowd just past the Stopper's shoulder.

"So annoying," I grumbled to myself, absentmindedly rubbing my chest.

Callie's warm hand landed on my arm, and I jerked at the touch. She gave me a knowing smile when I looked at her. Her eyes flicked to where my palm rested against my breastbone, and I yanked my hand away, feeling my face heat.

I looked up to see Puck purposely ignoring me, his jaw clenching as he looked toward Axel. Roko gave me a little cheers to try and pull me out of whatever my bond was doing right now.

"You're going to be great tomorrow." I bumped my glass with his, and we took a sip together.

"We're gonna kick some ass," he hollered, holding up his cup as the entire crowd cheered.

The pull in my chest made me stumble forward, and before I realized what I was doing, I found myself moving around my brother and Roko, past the Stopper who was pouring beer—and straight toward where Axel was standing. He wasn't facing me, but I couldn't take my eyes off the back of his head—I had to get there. It was the same draw I'd had before the Spring Equinox.

My breathing accelerated. I didn't want to be rejected again, but I couldn't stop. Axel stepped back from the group he was with and was promptly shoved to the side. A male bigger than anyone I'd ever seen jostled him out of the way. His eyes locked with mine, and it was like the world disappeared around us. I couldn't take my eyes off him as I moved forward, and he sped up, determined to get to me.

He was taller than any of my brothers and twice as wide as me. Even his muscles had muscles. His hair was golden brown, and he had the greenest eyes I'd ever seen. His skin was tan, and even though his features were boxy and hard with strength, he looked kind.

The warmest and most welcoming smile spread over his lips. He towered over me and wrapped his huge hands around my face.

"By the goddess, I've found you. I've envisioned this day and dreamed of you nightly. But my fantasy failed miserably, for you are even more beautiful than I could have ever imagined." His deep voice sunk into my bones, rattling me to my very core. "Tell me your name, my mate, and I will spend the rest of my life making all your dreams come true."

Reader's Note

Thank you for reading Summer Knights Dream! Your support means the world, and I look forward to sharing the rest of Lyra's story with you.

For the latest updates and news, be sure to follow me on social media at www.ariadnebreylard.com

Happy reading!

Ariadne

Acknowledgements

I extend my deepest gratitude to my incredible husband. Your unwavering support and encouragement have been my anchor throughout this literary adventure. Your belief in me has been invaluable, and I truly couldn't be more grateful for the constant strength you've provided.

To my children, your patience and understanding during late nights and the writing process have not gone unnoticed. You are my greatest creation. I love you to the farthest star and all the way back—times infinity.

To my beta readers, thank you for pointing out insights and offering constructive feedback, helping me see what I couldn't. To my street team, your passion for the characters and the story is beyond appreciated.

To the fans, your unwavering enthusiasm has made this journey all the more rewarding.

To the talented artists and diligent editors whose expertise has elevated the quality of this book.

I am sincerely grateful for each one of you.

Thank you,

Ariadne

Night Kingdom

Queen Hesper Araphel

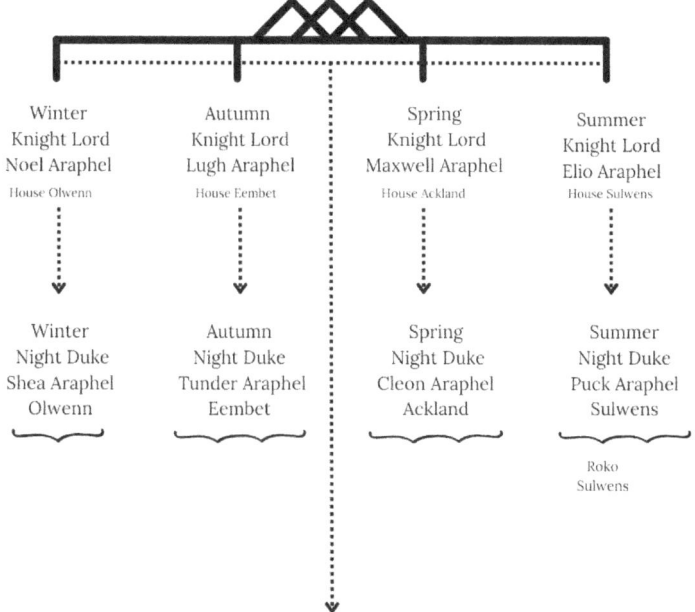

Winter	Autumn	Spring	Summer
Knight Lord	Knight Lord	Knight Lord	Knight Lord
Noel Araphel	Lugh Araphel	Maxwell Araphel	Elio Araphel
House Olwenn	House Eembet	House Ackland	House Sulwens

Winter	Autumn	Spring	Summer
Night Duke	Night Duke	Night Duke	Night Duke
Shea Araphel	Tunder Araphel	Cleon Araphel	Puck Araphel
Olwenn	Eembet	Ackland	Sulwens

Roko
Sulwens

Princess Lyra Araphel

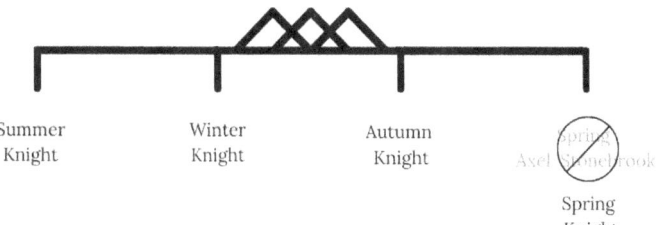

Summer	Winter	Autumn	Spring
Knight	Knight	Knight	Axel Stonebrook

Spring
Knight

- Lyra (*Leer-uh*) — Night Princess of the Night Kingdom
- Mother — Hesper — Queen of the Night Kingdom
- Father — Noel (NoUL) — Knight Lord of the Night Kingdom, from Winter Court
- Pai— Elio (*Eh-lee-oh*)— Knight Lord of the Night Kingdom, from Summer Court
- Baba— Lugh (LOO) — Knight Lord of the Night Kingdom, from Autumn Court
- Papa— Maxwell — Knight Lord of the Night Kingdom, from Spring Court
- Puck — Lyra's older brother, Night Duke of the Night Kingdom, Summer, Elio's son
- Shea — Lyra's older brother, Night Duke of the Night Kingdom, Winter, Noel's son
- Tunder — Lyra's older brother, Night Duke of the Night Kingdom, Spring, Maxwell's son
- Cleon — Lyra's older brother, Night Duke of the Night Kingdom, Autumn, Lugh's son
- High Priestess — Prophetess of Fate, Knight Kingdom
- Axel Stonebrook— Spring Court noble, rejected Lyra
- Roko (*Rock-oh*) — Puck's mate
- Callie — Summer Court, Lyra's best friend
- Professor Warrock — Economics Professor
- Jana — Axel's girlfriend
- Meira — Jana's friend
- Jed — Callie's friend from prep school
- Brev — Callie's friend from prep school
- Sidric — Callie's friend from prep school, Lyra's friend with benefits
- Landor — Axel's friend who was at the Spring Equinox
- Garret — youngest Day Lord, Lyra's first lover
- Mr. Gerk — Jed, Brev, Sidric, and Callie's prep school headmaster
- Malor — Black Squad's Waterback
- Lacy Ledark — Jana's friend

About the Author

Ariadne Breylard is an author with a passion for crafting fantasy romance novels that are both sweet and spicy. She resides in a beautiful mountainous region, where the natural surroundings provide endless inspiration for her writing.

With an infectious imagination and a love for all things fantastical, Ariadne weaves tales of epic love stories, enchanting worlds, and mythical creatures that leave readers spellbound.

Her captivating writing style has gained her a dedicated following of readers and won the hearts of fans worldwide, putting her books at the top of Amazon Best Seller Lists.

When she's not writing, Ariadne can be found tending to her garden, filled with an array of vibrant flowers and plants. She also enjoys spending time with her family, beloved animals, and listening to the enchanting melodies of neoclassical compositions.

If you enjoyed Ariadne Breylard's writing, explore more worlds crafted under the author's other pen names.

NVREADS.COM/NVP-PENNAMES